I0788526

Odo

By
C. S. Johns

Table of Contents

Dedications

i

This book is dedicated to my beloved grandmother,
Hazel Crooks Brown.

About the Author

C. S. Johns is a Southern boy and a proud Marine Corps veteran. Mexican food is his favorite food, and he can listen to blues music all day long. He prefers gloomy and rainy days over days of sunshine because it's more relaxing. He has recently found the love of his life and plans to get married in the near future.

Prologue

Since the beginning of time, the world has been plagued by demonic spirits and entities. Some terrorize and harm people, and some simply try to make their way back across from the world of the dead to the world of the living.

Western African countries such as Nigeria, Benin, and Togo have been terrorized by one of the most evil demonic spirits ever. This demon preys on the young, snatching children away from their parents, taking them to a secluded area and eventually killing them before devouring their bodies. At times, it doesn't devour its victims but uses them to capture a much younger victim. The younger the demon's victim is, the better because it gains strength from youth. Once the spirit chooses its victim, it will not stop until it gets what it wants.

The Yoruba people bravely try to fight it with amulets and simply keep their children in safe zones when they feel that the demon draws close. No one has ever seen it closely. It is believed that it can take many forms, sometimes multiple forms at once, so nobody knows exactly what the demon looks like. Nobody knows where it comes from… or how it finds us.

All we know is that it's called Abiku.

1
FAUSTIN

Lagos National Stadium/Lagos, Nigeria

A sea of people covered in red, green, blue, and yellow, moving in a wave-like motion, shouting incoherently. They all loudly sing in unison as the national flag of Nigeria floats throughout the crowd. The rumbles of the stadium sound like they would shatter every piece of cement that holds it steady. The eyes of the Nigerian fans look alarming, even crazed.

"Come on, Striker. Let's go," Faustin yells.

Another man slides in from the side, holding a couple of cups in his hands and has a seat.

"Where's mine?" Faustin huffs at his friend.

"You wanted some?" John jokingly asks. "Just kidding." He hands the steamy cup of Okro soup to Faustin and smirks. "It's about time our football team finally has potential."

"Our football team has always had potential. They just didn't have a coach." Faustin sips his soup.

John scoffs, "The other way around. Leeman was a better coach than this one."

"Do you remember Leeman's record?"

"Yes, I do. Because his players were idiots at first. He finally got some good players and had to step down." John points toward the Nigerian sidelines. "This man comes in to coach the players who Leeman brought in. They make him look good."

"Okay, let's agree to disagree." Faustin busts out laughing.

The crowd erupts in cheers.

"That was one of the good players." John points to the field.

"You've made your point."

There is a short pause in the conversation as they enjoy their soup.

"I hope you're ready for that 600 level." John sips his soup.

"After five years of headaches, keeping my face in those books, not having any kind of a life… Yes. If I'm not ready now, I'll never be ready," Faustin groans.

"That's good. I barely passed the 400-level medical exams," John said.

Faustin nudges John's arm. "But you got it. That's all that matters."

"Yep."

"I've applied for a position in America," Faustin added.

"Leaving Lagos? You're gonna leave me?" John sounds alert.

Faustin snickers. "No one's leaving you. There are plenty of positions open in America. You can apply to one of them."

"What does Jeanine think? Is she satisfied with being dragged away from her home?" John asks.

"My wife will do whatever I want her to do." Faustin jokingly puts his foot down. "Jeanine is quite satisfied. She plans to apply for a teaching position when we get there."

John nods.

"After the baby arrives, we'll head over there," Faustin continues to explain.

John pulls a small pack of candy from his pocket. "Do you know what you're having yet?"

Faustin freezes, noticing the candy. "Not yet. Whatever it is, I want a beautiful name… a strong name." He pauses for emphasis. "A name that can't be touched."

2
UMAR

Johns Hopkins Medical Center/Baltimore, Maryland

Dr. Umar Fulani, dressed for surgery, washes his hands all the way up to his elbows with the antibacterial soap that another team member pours from the side. He drys his hands and turns to another team member assisting him to don his surgical gown, then his scrubs, then his gloves.

The doctor speaks with a deep African accent. "Are the drapes set up correctly? Can everyone see the patient?"

Everyone nods and gets into position. One team member stands in front of the computer screen, monitoring it. Another team member directs a video camera on the patient.

"Everything is ready, Dr. Fulani." The team member clicks the camera on.

Dr. Fulani stands by the patient's head and leans into her. "We're going to do some drilling, sweetie. I want you to breathe easily. In through your nose and out through your mouth."

The buzzing sound of a drill starts. The team members watch.

"Good. Keep doing that." Dr. Fulani soothes the patient. "Open the electro."

"Now, we're going to do a few exercises. My assistant is going to hold some pictures up, and you tell me what you see."

The team member starts flipping the cards while the patient faintly responds. "Apple, banana, elephant, lion…"

"Good, very good." Dr. Fulani focuses on the patient's head.

Knowing the doctor's expertise, the patient's moans and groans don't seem to bother the staff in the room. They remain relaxed and professional.

"All finished." The doctor places the drill on the surgical table. "We're gonna wrap this up. You'll have to stay here for a while for observation."

"It's complete, Doctor." A team member by the computer punches a couple of buttons on the keyboard.

"Good. Send it to me, and I'll take a look." The doctor exits the room to go to his office. He sits down in his cozy chair, clicks a few buttons, and starts to analyze the recorded brain activity slowly. Pointing and whispering to himself, he starts to jot down little notes about what he sees.

A knock on the door distracts him from the screen. "Come in!"

The team member opens the door, looking disgruntled. "The patient is complaining that I'm harassing her. She asked to see you."

Keeping his eyes on the computer screen, Dr. Fulani sighs and then brushes it off. "It's natural. Over the next twenty-four hours, keep asking her basic questions. It's critical to her recovery. She complains now, but she'll be thankful later."

He continues to visually dissect the brain through the computer screen while his cell phone begins to vibrate on the desk.

"Yes?" he answers.

After listening, he remains calm. "What? What happened? Again? Is he still there?"

Biting his lip and rolling his eyes, chides himself. "Fuck! Fuck!"

He cuts his eyes over to a well-organized book stand and focuses on one book in particular, the *Holy Bible*. He stares at it as though he's either looking for help or answers.

3
UMAR

Paul Laurence Dunbar High School

Dr. Fulani pulls into a school parking lot with his fancy white Audi Prestige and exits the vehicle. He makes his way through a thick crowd of students lingering outside of the school who are smoking and joking. The hallways are packed full of students scurrying to their next class. Dr. Fulani almost has to navigate through it sideways.

He enters the secretary's office as she sits at her desk. She swivels in her chair to greet him. "Good Morning Doctor—." He cuts her off with a quick hello and keeps walking without even looking her way.

Bursting into the principal's office without knocking, a middle-aged white man with a sagging scowl on his face sits behind his desk, which looks to be very eroded and held together by termites. Sitting directly across from the white man is a fresh-faced young black boy. The boy's demeanor looks a little hardened for his fourteen-year-old age.

"Dad! This man…" The boy looks up at Dr. Fulani.

Dr. Fulani holds his finger up toward his son while he breathes deeply with his nostrils flaring. "Shut up!"

The middle-aged principal sits calmly. "Dr. Fulani, as you well know, this isn't the first or the second time your son has been caught with something that he isn't supposed to have in school."

"I know." The doctor has a seat.

The principal releases a stressed sigh. "First, it was the marijuana. Not much, but enough. I didn't make a big deal about it because I know how kids are today. And besides, I smoked a little bit of reefer back in the day. We only suspended him for a few days for the incident. The second time was a picture of one of his little fourteen-year-old classmates lifting her shirt and exposing her breasts. He was trying to sell it. That's distribution of child pornography, and it almost made me get the police involved."

Dr.Fulani sits, silently pissed off, as he clenches his jaw and tightens his fists. One can almost see the steam rising off of his head.

The boy smirks arrogantly. "Funny, that picture just disappeared. What'd you do with it, Garrard?"

"Franklin, shut up." The doctor throws his finger in his son's face.

"But this time, a knife. That's dangerous," Principal Garrad explains.

The doctor turns back to the principal. "How'd you find out he had a knife?"

"He got into a little argument with another classmate. They were about to start fighting, and one of the other kids heard him say that he would carve him up."

Dr. Fulani stares at his son. Franklin shifts away, trying to avoid eye contact.

"Where's the knife?" Dr. Fulani asks.

The principal reaches into his drawer and pulls out a very large Bowie hunting knife. "A simple pocket knife is bad enough, but this is like a freaking machete. Thank God that it wasn't a gun."

"I can assure you this will never happen again," the doctor implores.

The principal slightly shakes his head. "I've heard that before. With the drugs, the photo of the young girl, and now this… It's the third strike."

"What are you saying?" The doctor looks confused, but deep down inside, he knows what's going to be said next.

"We have no choice but to expel him from this school."

The doctor's tone escalates. "Are you serious? All of the money that I've put into this school. I've donated money for that new cafeteria and to help with upgrading the new library. Your football team is now playing on a decent field."

Principal Garrard interrupts quickly but in a quiet manner. "I know. And I brought those things up to the board, but they said that this is too much."

Doctor Fulani rolls his eyes toward his son and shakes his head in shame. "You did this. Remember that."

4
UMAR

Fulani Residence

The doctor is cozy in his high-end Spanish-style home decorated with his posh layered lighting, beautiful marble fireplace, metallic decor items, and large wall art.

No matter how much luxury is in the house, the extravagant glow is kept at a minimum by the sight of the typical teenage things placed in the most random spots. Sneakers on the steps, a baseball bat against the staircase, and a football in the middle of the floor.

A woman in her mid-forties is in the kitchen washing some dirty dishes. She's dressed down with black sweatpants and a t-shirt but dons an African head wrap on her head. She carries the grace and elegance of an African queen. Dr. Fulani sneaks up behind her and gives her a peck on the cheek.

Josephine jumps and giggles. "Don't sneak on me like that, I told you to pull him out of that school a long time ago. There's nothing but trouble at that school, and I don't like the kids he hangs around."

The doctor relaxes at the kitchen table. "Well, it seems like the whole damn school is crap. They have all kinds of dirt from all kinds of students there, but all they want to focus on are his screwups."

He sits at the table, sighing.

"Maybe this is a blessing," Josephine adds.

"It doesn't make any sense. After all of the money I put into that school, Franklin should be the last one they kick out."

Josephine speaks unruffled about the situation, "You know they've given him too many chances already."

Dr. Fulani starts shuffling through a thick pile of mail on the table, flicking one after another to the side as if none of it has any importance. The majority of the mail is posted from Nigeria. "Have you heard from your sister?"

"I talked to her this morning?"

"How is the family? They're still moving here, right?" His eyes are focused on mail from Lagos.

"They can't wait." Josephine smiles.

Dr. Fulani nods. "Good. They can put that boy in a good school with Franklin."

Josephine turns with an idea. "Roosevelt—"

Her husband interrupts, "Oh, he is definitely going to Roosevelt tomorrow. I don't care if he has a problem with being around a lot of white kids and that he will be one of the only black faces in the school."

A lawn mower revs up outside and catches Dr. Fulani's attention. He takes a gaze outside and sees a white man in his mid-forties with scruffy-looking facial hair and dingy weekend clothes used to do housework. The white man waves through the window at the onlooking doctor.

Dr. Fulani stares through the window. "He'd better enjoy the day out of school today as much as he can because tomorrow he's going right back in… but Roosevelt this time."

The doctor turns to his wife and caresses her. "I have to get back to the office now. I told them I'd be gone for only about one hour." He checks his watch. "It's been almost three hours now."

He gives her a peck on the lips and exits the house. He steps along his spotless rubber pavers that are tucked in between two long limestone flower beds of thick hydrangea flowers. The freshly cut lawn is smoothly designed with a soft wave style.

The lawn-mowing neighbor cuts off the machine. "Howdy, neighbor!"

"Hey, Curtis. It must be nice to be retired." Dr Fulani waves.

Curtis takes a big whiff of the fresh air and looks around at his new freedom.

"You have no idea. Don't have to worry about moving from my bed until I'm ready. Don't have to worry about shoveling down my breakfast to be on time for anything. I can actually sit and enjoy taking my time. You'll have your day soon."

"Not soon enough," Dr. Fulani replies.

"How goes the fight?"

Dr. Fulani snickers. "Which one?"

Curtis wipes the sweat from his brow. "The fight against death. The fight to help people live longer. Is there any other one?"

The doctor shrugs and looks away. Curtis immediately recognizes the sign that there are other issues brewing in the Fulani family.

"Oh! Franklin having problems at school again?"

"The fight at work continues, but the fight with my son's school problems has ended. He's getting enrolled at Roosevelt tomorrow," the doctor assures.

The exhilaration in Curtis's voice elevates. "That's what I'm talking about. One hell of a school there. Many district titles in basketball… several state titles in football."

"And one hell of an academic program." Dr. Fulani interrupts.

"Yeah, I was going to say that too."

The doctor snickers and shakes his head before continuing the casual stroll to his car. Curtis continues to yell with excitement, "Great soccer team. The wrestling team is top-tier. The debate team isn't so bad, either. Roosevelt's my alma mater, ya know?"

Dr. Fulani throws his hand in the air, waving goodbye. He rounds the corner of his car and opens the door while taking a quick glance back at the house. He does a double-take and freezes, noticing Franklin staring out of the upstairs window with a menacing stare. The doctor shrugs it off and hops into his car.

5
FAUSTIN

Ikeja Lagos Neighborhood/Nwaike Residence

Faustin sits at an old desk in a sunlit room with his face buried in a book. The only light coming into the room is from the opened curtains, displaying the emptiness of his surroundings. Everything is packed up in the dusty boxes scattered in the room, with the exception of the lone desk and chair. The dust particles of the area can be seen floating within the ray of light shooting through the window.

A young African woman in her late twenties sneaks up behind him and plants a soft kiss on the back of his head. She looks to be about nine months pregnant.

"Mata Na!" He turns and smiles.

She gently rubs his shoulders and upper chest to try to soothe his studying stress. "Masoyina! You're the hardest-working man I've ever known. Give it a rest for a little while."

"Don't worry, Jeanine. I will be done soon enough."

"I don't want you stressing too much over this. I don't need my husband dropping dead of a heart attack and leaving me here to raise a child by myself," Jeanine explains.

Faustin snickers and shakes his head. "You're putting a little too much on it, don't you think?"

She smacks her lips and gives a playful shove. "No!"

"So dramatic. Is this a part of that hormone thing?" Faustin giggles. "When it is all over, we'll throw a nice party to relax."

Jeanine's worries ease a little, hearing about the upcoming plans to de-stress.

Faustin turns back to his book. "We'll have a few friends over."

"Not John." She pauses.

Slightly confused, Faustin slowly turns back around. "And what's wrong with my friend?"

She stares at him for a moment, wondering why he doesn't understand her discomfort about his friend.

"What's wrong with him? I don't think anyone at the party wants to constantly have necklaces with creepy charms pushed in their faces all night," Jeanine explains.

Faustin rolls his eyes. "It's a little extra money that he's trying to make. I thought you liked jewelry anyway?"

She starts shuffling through some of the old boxes. "Not those. And they come from his uncle's shop. That makes it worse."

"Yes, I know you think all amulet makers are weird."

Faustin turns around again, and Jeanine places herself on his lap. He gently rubs her pregnant stomach and starts playful purring like a cat.

"When little Odo comes, I think he will be a blessing from the sky." Faustin plays with her stomach.

She jumps slightly. "Odo?"

"Yes."

The faint sound of wind chimes tinkle from outside of the window, and it catches their attention. Faustin rises up and takes a glance through the window. The yard is riddled with specially made wind chimes that look like they've been put together in a small tinker toy shop. All of them are double-headed axes.

Faustin gazes through the window. "Ahh, Oshe, the thunder god, is making some noise, letting us know he's still here protecting the house."

He takes a couple of seconds for a few deep breaths, relishing the peaceful moment provided by yard ornaments of his mythical Yaruban god.

He gives his wife a light slap on the ass. "Well, it's now or never.

She lays a soft kiss on his lips. "Good luck."

Faustin grabs his backpack and slings it over his shoulder before heading out the door. They wave their goodbyes to each other.

He sits in his college classroom. It's a pretty spacious class where students are able to sit spaced apart for testing purposes. Around the class, there are human body model samples in the posterior position. In the back of the class are daily medical classwork aids, such as microscopes, stethoscopes, and beaker cylinders all covered up and put to the side.

The professor, in his late fifties and dressed in a nice button-down and a tie, casually zigzags through the classroom, dropping booklets on the desks in front of his students. He seems pretty stern and professional, so much so that his presence intimidates the students.

Faustin's very fidgety and can't stop glancing all around from the nerves jumping in his body. He constantly adjusts in his seat while the muscles in his body twitch. He can feel his heart beating through his chest.

The professor continues to walk. "If you thought the previous exams were difficult—300 level, 400 level, 500 level—you will not have as much success with this one. That's most, if not all, of you. There are some here who will not pass this one. That happens every year."

A booklet is slapped on the desk in front of Fasutin. He jumps slightly but keeps it under control. His edginess goes unnoticed by everyone around him. But he notices some students' edginess around him.

The professor continues his casual stroll. "The 600-level exam is one of the most difficult in the world. But don't worry, you have exactly five hours to complete it… Starting now.

Faustin anxiously flips open his booklet. The wall clock reads 8:30, and over time, the full class starts to decrease little by little as students fade away. Faustin still sits among the remaining students.

Another male student sits, staring at his test paper. He cautiously glances left and then right. He opens his hands to take a quick and discreet peek at the small slip of paper in his palm before he hears a grunting sound coming from over his shoulder. He closes his eyes tight and bows his head in shame before he looks up because he knows that he was caught cheating.

"You are excused. Thank you." The professor snatches the exam away.

Faustin witnesses the cheater caught in the act and rolls his eyes back to his test. He starts jotting on the paper while the ticking of the clock echoes into a slow fade.

6
FAUSTIN

Ikeja Lagos Neighborhood/Nwaike Residence

The neighborhood is dark except for the light from the Nwaike house shining through the windows. There's a lot of activity packed inside. Large clusters of partiers chitchat with drinks in their hands. The chatter is incoherent. A banner on the wall reads, "Congratulations Dr. Nwaike!"

Faustin and John stand in the kitchen, isolating conversation from the rest of the bunch.

John seems filled with excitement as he reaches into the refrigerator and grabs two Heinekens. "So how does it feel? Huh? Doctor?"

Faustin grabs the beer that John holds out. "To tell you the truth, it feels… relieving. Relieved that I don't have to worry about tests anymore. How do you feel?"

John takes a sip. "Ahh! You have many jokes. I won't take mine for another couple of months. I still have to stress a little."

Faustin snickers, "I think you'll have a much easier time than I did. You've always been a better test taker than me."

Jeanine walks in and gives her husband a peck on the lips. John displays a little playful jealousy. "Where's mine?"

Faustin and Jeanine turn and give John a stare. John shakes his head.

Jeanine gives a gentle rub on Faustin's cheek. "I'm so proud of my love. John, aren't you proud of him too?"

John nods while taking a sip of his Heineken.

Jeanine gives a couple of soft slaps on Faustin's cheek. "He's going to be the best doctor at Johns Hopkins."

Jeanine walks out and back into the company of the rest of their visitors. John very cautiously studies her departure from the room and slowly reaches into his pocket to pull out a silver necklace with an amulet charm.

The charm looks to be a small figure of a cartoonish man with small spikes protruding out of his torso all around. It's very old and rusted looking and bears no astonishing features. John finds the charms captivating, and his eyes are locked in on it as he holds it up to Faustin's face.

Faustin shakes his head. "No… no."

"It's a going away gift. It's also for a little luck," John explains.

Faustin hesitates, knowing how Jeanine feels about John's jewelry. "What kind of spell did your grandfather put on it?"

They pause, staring at each other. John twists his lips in wonder. John grabs ahold of Faustin's hand and dangles the necklace over the palm.

"Take that voodoo out of my house!" Jeanine yells as she looks on from the background.

They snatch their hands away to attempt to hide the already-noticed jewelry.

"Wha… What voodoo?" John stammers.

Jeanine pouts aggressively, walks up to John, and snatches the necklace from his hands.

"This voodoo…" She holds the necklace up.

Faustin holds a slight look of embarrassment on his face while John huffs and puffs with annoyance.

John pleads, "But it will protect you."

"I don't want it here," Jeanine insists.

John sighs and looks at both of them before walking out of the kitchen. "Sorry!"

Jeanine focuses her aggression on Faustin. "I cannot believe you."

"What?"

"You know what."

Faustin snickers and reaches out to his wife while she still pouts. "Come here."

They find comfort in each other's arms.

Later that night, as the company of the party leaves, Faustin and Jeanine stand in the doorway waving goodbye. They shut the door, and Jeanine notices that John is still on the couch, kicking back with his feet up on the table.

"Um… what are you still doing here?" Jeanine folds her arms.

Faustin strolls over to have a seat. "Come on. He's my company. We're going to relax and watch a little television."

Jeanine walks away, rolling her eyes.

"I gotta use the bathroom." John rises up and starts to walk out of the room.

"You know where it is." Faustin's eyes are fixated on the bright television screen.

John walks into the hallway and notices a black backpack in the corner on the floor. His eyes quickly scan around for anyone watching. He unzips the front pouch, pulls the necklace from his pocket, and slides it inside. He carefully places the backpack back in the corner, trying to make it look as if the bag wasn't moved at all.

In the kitchen, Jeanine walks in and prepares to clean the stacks of dirty dishes from the party. The window is cracked open, and the curtains give an easy wave from the wind blowing. She rubs her pregnant stomach gently and gives a soft giggle.

"Kicking, are we?" she says quietly to the unborn.

The curtains jump from an abnormally strong gust of wind from the outside. Jeanine leans over the sink and takes a cautious gaze through the window. She sees nothing.

In the bathroom, John is letting it flow into the toilet. He finishes, flushes, then washes his hands.

"Yes, you do look good." He checks himself out in the mirror.

A faint humming sound hits his ears, but he can't tell where it's coming from. The sound, not getting any louder, seems to be directed from the drain, so he leans in. He opens the cabinet under the sink to take a look, and the humming stops.

In the living room, Faustin continues to lounge while watching television. He quietly chuckles at the show that's showing.

John walks back in. "It's a good thing you're leaving here. Make sure the person who buys this house next knows about those shitty bathroom sink pipes."

"What are you talking about? There is nothing wrong with my sink pipes," Faustin assures.

"If you say so. I have to go, brother." He gives Faustin a rub on the top of the head.

"You're going already?"

John puts Faustin's tensions at ease. "I'll be back in the morning to help you pack some things."

Faustin gets up and walks his friend to the door. John yells to Jeanine, "Bye, Jeanine. I'll be back in the morning."

Jeanine yells from the kitchen, "Bye, John. Don't be in such a rush to come back.

John and Faustin give each other a little fist bump before John exits.

John descends the porch steps, walks down the walkway, and steps out of the already-opened fence gate. He gets to his car and starts to shuffle through the different keys on his keychain. Far in the background stands an unknown figure in the tree line. The figure is of a human but could be either a man or a woman. The figure stands motionless, watching John's every move. He stays oblivious to his surroundings, hops into his car and pulls off.

In the house, Faustin picks up a few things along with the black backpack on the floor and throws them into an empty moving box. Jeanine washes dishes, and all that he sees through the kitchen window is blackness as the curtains continue to wave softly. There is an ominous feeling that something is there, but it hides quietly in the darkness. She rubs her stomach from the baby kicking. A faint, raspy voice leaks through the window, speaking incoherently. Suddenly worried, Jeanine clutches her stomach in pain. Faustin enters the kitchen and catches her in his arms before she hits the floor.

"I think it's time." Jeanine cringes.

Faustin's eyes become almost twice the size they normally are as he scrambles to get Jeanine to her feet. His anxiousness causes him to lose almost all sense of awareness as he scrambles everywhere to look for the car keys that are on the countertop. He snatches the keys and slings Jeanine's arm over his shoulder to help her to the front door.

Outside, he slams the passenger car door shut and scurries around to the driver's side, giggling like a little schoolgirl. His nervousness causes his hands to tremble to the point of not being able to hold the keys steady in his hand. He drops the keys and then picks them up while taking a split-second deep breath to gain some steadiness. He hops into the car, where Jeanine is panting in labor.

Faustin puts his cell phone up to his ear and waits. John picks up from the other end of the call. "Yes, man?"

"She's having it now. We're headed to the hospital," Faustin babbles.

"Now? I'll meet you there."

They hang up, and Faustin's face has glee splattered all over it while Jeanine continues to pant.

In John's car, he hangs up the phone and has a serious look of concern on his face.

7
FAUSTIN

Reddington Hospital

In the hospital, Jeanine sits in a wheelchair while Faustin zigzags through the thick traffic of patients, doctors, and nurses. He almost runs a couple of people over. There are shouts, complaints, and curse words hurled toward them.

A nurse sits behind the check-in counter, filling out some paperwork. Faustin slams his body into the counter, trying to quickly grab her attention. She almost jumps out of her seat. Faustin leans on the counter and can barely stand from the exhaustion, but the adrenaline keeps him going.

He huffs and heaves, barely able to speak. "We… need… a… doctor. In the delivery room, a nurse snatches the curtain closed, and the doctor positions himself in between Jeanine's spread legs. She screams in agony. Faustin holds his wife's hand and pats her brow with a damp washcloth to comfort her.

"Come on, push! You have to push!" the doctor urges.

Jeanine grunts and growls with heavy pants mixed in.

Faustin speaks soothingly to her. "We will attend football games, school dances, everything."

"I see a head. A couple more pushes," the doctor insists.

The nurse hands the doctor the forceps while Jeanine gives more grunts and blows.

The doctor asks, "Father, do you want to see your child coming into the world?"

"Hell no. I mean, no, thank you. I'll see him when he gets out." Faustin explains not being able to stand seeing a birth.

The doctor gives a slight chuckle. "A lot of men can't bear the sight of a birth. It's natural."

Jeanine gives a long, exhausted grunt before hearing the cries of a newborn baby.

"Say hello to your son." The doctor observes the baby and hands him to the nurse.

The nurse wipes the newborn off while the doctor grabs the hemostat and clamps before using the sponge.

Later, in the hospital labor and delivery room, Jeanine lies in the bed, holding the baby with Faustin by her side. The baby wiggles around in its wraps as they kiss and caress it. The tiny grunts of a newborn can be heard.

"Ah, yes! You did well. He is the most beautiful thing I've seen," Faustin whispers, trying not to startle the baby.

Jeanine looks at Faustin. "Well, do you have a name for your son?"

"He's so young, so beautiful, so strong. I think Odo is the name for him." Faustin gently tickles the baby's wraps.

Jeanine turns to look at the baby and contemplates. "Odo? I like it."

There is a slight flicker of the light with a quick and faint buzz from them. The new parents look around in confusion.

Naturally reacting as a protector, Jeanine pulls the child in closer and shields it with her hand. "What is that?"

Faustin quickly brushes the flicker off like it's nothing. "Sometimes these old hospitals are not wired correctly."

The curtain is almost completely closed, with the exception of a small crack. The feeling of being watched causes Faustin's eyes to slowly navigate toward the crack. Through it, there is one eye that stares back. Its trance-like glare sends a chilling feeling into the room.

Faustin cautiously speaks. "Hello?"

The eye doesn't move. The eye doesn't blink. The eye doesn't even squint or respond in any way.

A few seconds float by before the curtains are snatched open, revealing a nurse with a crooked smile. She doesn't look as professional or well-kept as the other nurses, but she still dons a clean uniform.

The nurse starts to slowly walk in, "Hello. I was checking to see if you needed anything."

Jeanine stays oblivious to the creepiness of the nurse. "No, thank you. We're okay at the moment."

Faustin brushes off the previous eerie moment and starts to approach the nurse. "Yes, we are great. This hospital has one of the most professional staffs I have been around."

The nurse's eyes widen as she notices the newborn. Faustin holds out his hand to shake the nurse's hand, but she's locked in on the baby and nothing else. She slowly walks past Faustin's hand as if he were invisible. Inching closer and closer to the little bundle of joy in Jeanine's arms, Jeanine becomes a little nervous and squeezes the baby tighter.

John bursts into the room. He's breathing heavily and sweating profusely. The nurse's attention snaps around to John as she starts to approach him.

"Where have you been?" Faustin's attention also turns to John.

John, trying to catch his breath, is barely able to talk. "I'm so sorry. I… tried to get here earlier, but I got held up. I had to…"

John is distracted when the nurse approaches with awkward dismay. She moves to within inches of his face and quietly studies him. John is completely frozen, wondering what the hell she is doing. He eyes back and forth to Faustin and Jeanine as they look the same way.

"How are you? Can I help you?" John leans back slightly, attempting to keep somewhat of a safe distance.

The nurse's nostrils flare from taking a couple of sniffs. She makes a face of disgust.

"Not anymore." She cuts quickly to the side and walks out without looking back.

John takes a couple of sniffs of himself and shrugs it off.

One of the nurses from the delivery pokes her head into the room. "I was checking to see if you need anything."

Faustin smiles. "No, thank you. The other nurse already asked."

"What other nurse?" She looks back in the hallway.

"The one who was here before you," he added.

The nurse has a look of confusion on her face. "I'm the only nurse assigned to you."

"Maybe it was a nurse who was assigned to someone else, and she was being nice," Jeanine added.

"Well, let me know if you need anything. I'll be in and out." The nurse steps out.

Fautin smiles. "I think the other nurse had a thing for you, John."

Faustin and Jeanine snicker.

"She's not my type. Not even close." John gets upset.

"Not your type? Okay. It's about time you have a little one yourself." Faustin gives a gentle tug on the baby's soft wraps.

Feeling that the conversation would go nowhere, John quickly changes the subject. "Okay, I'll take the first watch. You rest and relax…"

Faustin interrupts the seemingly over-protective John. "Wait. First watch? Don't start that crazy talk."

"Here we go again." Jeanine rolls her eyes.

"I'm saying we have to protect the child," John insists.

Faustin elevates his voice. "For the last time, nothing is going to happen to our child. Look around. It is a hospital. There is no one dangerous here."

John flops down in the corner chair and drops his head in his hands, very disappointed.

"What is it that you are afraid of? Who is supposed to be coming to take my child?" Jeanine asks.

"He thinks the Abiku is coming," Faustin scoffs.

Jeanine looks confused, "What?"

Surprised, John lifts his head out of his hands and stares at Jeanine.

"I'm sorry. I've never heard of the Abiku," Jeanine adds.

"My grandfather told me the story of the Abiku when I was younger," John drops his hands.

"I've heard of it but have never heard the story," Faustin says.

John gently rubs the palms of his hands together, "It was in the 15th century. Some Christian missionaries built a school in Benin. That was the first time anyone had seen missionaries, so the villagers were fascinated by what they were teaching. The royal family at the time was the Futu Empire. Little by little they started to convert to Christianity and were helping to spread the message through the country. The military general who was a houngan in Voodoo."

"What is that?" Jeanine asks.

"A high priest," Faustin answers.

Johns continues his story, "The general was not happy with the spread of this religion, so he and his followers snuck into the Futu's kingdom and simultaneously slaughtered them all. He sent a message out to all Christian followers that they would be beheaded if they continued these practices. Several families were captured and mutilated. One family was captured and had a little eight-year-old girl named Abidemi. This girl was very much into Christianity, and she carried her bible everywhere she went. One night, when she and her family were bound to the cages that were made from the toughest African bamboo, Abika approached her from the shadows.

"Do you mean Abiku?" Jeanine asked.

John continues, "No, Abika. He's one of the angels that fell with Lucifer. If you know the story, you would know that Lucifer was thrown down with one-third of the angels. Abika was one of them. He approached little Abidemi with a proposition of having her and her family freed and kill her capturers if she would do his evil deeds. She agreed and was immediately set free. Later, a massive pile of body parts and limbs were found with the general's decapitated head on top of the pile. Through the years, little Abidemi grew up having Abika constantly approach her to give her orders to kill. She started to feel that her childhood had been stolen from her by Abika, so she turned her back on his orders and set out to destroy the youth of Africa. Abika felt betrayed and cursed her with eternal suffering, only to grow weaker and more grotesque if she doesn't feed."

Faustin stands stunned while Jeanine shakes her head.

"Rest, John. If someone comes into the hospital to try to steal the baby, there are nurses and doctors everywhere, as well as security. No one is going to feed on my child," Jeanine reassures.

"You know that you are not going to be able to go to America as soon as you think. You cannot travel with the child," John sighs.

"Yes, we have to wait about a couple of months. Already have it planned," Faustin assures.

All of a sudden, John displays a look of confusion on his face as if in deep thought. He takes a glance back toward the closed curtain and then turns back to continue thinking. He shrugs whatever he was thinking off and leans back in the chair, closing his eyes.

The clock on the wall reads 8:00 and slowly fades to 9:15. John opens his eyes and notices Jeanine sound asleep in the bed and the newborn sleeping next to the bed in the hospital bassinet. Faustin is nowhere to be seen.

He quietly grunts as he rises from the chair and exits the room.

John leisurely walks down the hospital hallway. The place seems as if it has been completely deserted because there is absolutely no movement. It's complete silence, with the exception of John's shoes clacking on the shiny museum-like marble floor and the faint buzzing of some of the lights. Every corner and every intersection that he passes, he hopes to see or hear another person, but the loneliness of his journey only continues.

He opens the glass door to the hospital cafeteria room and approaches a vending machine. Fiddling around with change in his pocket, a blurry figure slowly slides in the background, but on the other side of the glass wall. It watches John closely.

John drops the coins into the machine and presses the coffee button. The coffee slowly dribbles out, and John obliviously watches the coffee drip instead of noticing that he's being watched.

He very lowly whistles a fine tune and stretches a little to wake himself up more. Rolling his neck to stretch, he looks around and behind him. He doesn't see anything or anyone watching him from outside of the glass because the figure is not there anymore.

He turns back around and grabs his coffee before taking a relieving sip. The rising steam smothers his face as he closes his eyes for a moment of relaxation.

Focusing on the details of his cup of coffee, he exits the food and lodging room. A hand quickly reaches in and grabs his shoulder. Alarmed, some of the coffee spills from the cup as John's body reacts to the sudden scare. It's the nurse who was assigned to Jeanine's delivery.

"What are you doing here? You can't be here. Visiting hours are over." The nurse pulls her hand away from John's shoulder.

John pants a little from the scare. "Okay."

"John?" Faustin comes walking down the hallway.

"Where were you?" John looks back and forth between him and the nurse.

"I had to use the restroom," Faustin responded.

The nurse looks at Faustin. "Your friend cannot be here."

"I know. He was about to leave." Faustin jerks his head in a direction while looking at John.

John continues to sip on his freshly bought coffee, "No, I wasn't."

Faustin slings his arm around John's neck and playfully pulls him along. "Yes, you were. Thank you for coming. I will stay here all night."

John's concerns rise. "Are you going to stay up all night?"

Faustin rolls his eyes and sends out a sigh of annoyance. "Goodbye, John."

John hangs his head low and walks out of the building with a slight pout as if he were a child. Crickets chirp in the night, and the gravel crunches under his feet as he walks. Everything else is perfectly still as he hops into his car, takes a quick glance in the back seat and adjusts his rearview mirror. The car slowly pulls off while Faustin watches from behind the glass hospital door.

Jeanine lies in the bed, sound asleep, while the baby lies next to her in the bassinet. Faustin tiptoes in, trying to be as quiet as possible, and gives the baby a soft peck on the head. He quietly creeps around the bed and gives Jeanine a similar kiss, and she opens her eyes.

"Shh! I didn't mean to wake you up," Faustin whispers in Jeanine's face.

She grunts a little, adjusting herself to a more comfortable position. "It's fine. What time is it?"

Faustin gently strokes her hair. "Late. Too late for you to be awake. You should be motionless like little Odo over there."

They take a few moments gazing into each other's eyes and enjoying the rare peaceful moments as new parents.

"John went home?" she murmurs.

"Yes, he left."

Jeanine snickers and shakes her head at John's weird ways. "That man is so paranoid."

Faustin snickers back. "I kind of understand his concern. My grandfather used to tell me stories about that. I've always pushed it aside, not really thinking about it."

"Your grandfather?" she calmly whispers.

Faustin reflects deeply. "Yes. He was a crazy man but a good man. He used to tell me these stories about when he was younger, and the family had to fight off this demon when my father was born."

Jeanine lies there staring into her husband's eyes as he ponders.

"This demon is supposed to take children away," Faustin adds.

"To where?" Jeanine's eyes drop down a little as her mind imagines.

He shrugs. "I don't know, but supposedly, when it chooses a family, it won't move on to another family until it successfully snatches someone. I don't remember experiencing anything when I was a child, but my grandfather told me that we never know which generation it will come back for next."

"And John has it in his mind that it will come back for little Odo?" Jeanine's curiosity rises.

"I guess. But I was told that the only way it could touch anyone in the family was to be personally welcomed into the home by the head of the household. It can make its way into your home, but it cannot touch anyone," Faustin explains.

Jeanine scoffs and washes it away as if it's a joke. "Simply don't invite it into the house."

Faustin's eyebrows rise. "I was thinking the same thing, but then I remembered he told me that no one knows what it looks like. Over time, those stories kind of faded away from me because I have three younger sisters who were born after me. Nothing out of the ordinary has ever happened when they were born, and we've invited plenty of people into our home when I was growing up. A lot of them I've never seen before, so I think those are just stories."

Meanwhile, John steers slowly down a dimly lit two-way road. The soft rumble of the engine and the crunching of the occasional piece of loose gravel make for a very smooth journey. His vision starts to fade into blurriness, and his eyelids become like weights as he exerts more effort into keeping them up. He constantly shakes his head to keep himself somewhat alert. The soft ambient music playing on the radio and the raindrops starting to hit the windshield don't make matters any better.

He turns on the windshield wipers and changes the tunes as the headlights from constant oncoming traffic almost blind him. "The last thing I need to help me stay awake. Turn it on something else."

He reaches down to adjust the soft tunes and freezes, noticing out of the corner of his eye a pair of legs of someone in the passenger's seat. He doesn't know what to make of it and slowly scans up to the casually sitting body that's covered in a dried-up, blood-smeared hospital gown.

Before he can see the face of the person, an oncoming vehicle aggressively honks a warning. John quickly snaps his head back toward the front, and a loud crash of a wreck vibrates everything within a mile radius.

As the wall clock reads a quarter until midnight, Jeanine peacefully sleeps in the bed, while Faustin slouches in the nearby chair, covered in a blanket. The tiny babbles and coos of the newborn come from the bassinet. White nurses' shoes slowly creep through the curtain and cautiously approach the bassinet. The ankles are very thin and frail, with thin veins being strangled by the skin around them. The ankles seem to barely be able to pick the shoes up off of the ground.

Faustin's nostrils flare from his breathing while the babbles, and coos mix in with a very faint and almost incoherent raspy voice. "Shhhh! Little babies should be sleeping."

The white shoes scurry back through the curtains, which close a split-second before Faustin's eyes open. He notices the curtain moving slightly as if someone had walked through them. The baby grows silent, so he shifts his attention to the bassinet and quickly jumps out of the chair to lunge over to it, only to see the newborn wiggling around. He breathes a huge, silent sigh of relief.

8
FAUSTIN

Reddington Hospital/Discharge

The clock reads 10:30 a.m. Faustin lies partially on the bed and playfully teases the baby while Jeanine holds him. The normally closed curtain is wide open to the world, and all of the actions of the hospital employees can be seen.

The nurse walks in. She speaks extremely softly and politely. "Well, you both will be going home today with your new love."

Faustin rises out of the bed with a big smile on his face. "Yes, we already have everything set up there. The room is covered with elephants for my baby boy."

"Elephants?" The nurse's eyebrows rise.

Jeanine bounces the baby in her arms, "Yes. he has blue wallpaper with elephants covering the walls and stuffed elephants everywhere."

Faustin stands there with a big look of glee on his face.

"If we were having a girl, he was going to do all pink with hippos," she added.

The nurse smiles. "I would have loved that room when I was younger. I'm sure your son will love it."

Faustin leans in and gives the nurse a hug. "I can't begin to tell you how nice you have been to us."

"It's a part of my job," she giggles and hugs him back.

He gives a long and drawn-out squeeze, really showing appreciation for her hospitality.

"The doctor will get your release papers prepared so that you can be on your way." She squeezes him back.

The nurse walks out of the room, and Faustin starts to pack some personal belongings that were brought to the hospital while Jeanine continues to caress the baby.

On the way home, it's a nice, quiet ride with Jeanine in the passenger's seat. Gazing out of the window. The baby sleeps in the car seat in the back seat. A little stunned, Faustin leans in and gets a better look through the front windshield. Shards of glass and small pieces of a vehicle are scattered all over the road. It looks like enough of it has been cleaned up to where the vehicle cannot be recognized.

Faustin leans in. "Wow! It looks like there was an accident or something."

Jeanine studies the wreckage, "Yes, I see."

Faustin slows the car down to take a closer look at the damage. He slowly scans, looking for anything and everything that would help him recognize the type of vehicle it was. All he sees are small parts of side-view mirrors, metal pieces of the bumper, and strips of torn tires. Nothing stands out to him, so he shrugs it off and keeps pushing forward, speeding the car up.

Inside the Nwaike residence, blotches of the interior are lit up by the sunlight shooting through the windows. The moving shadows on the wooden floor are coming from the outside. The door swings open, and in walks Jeanine holding little Odo wrapped up. Faustin clumsily walks in after, struggling to carry the bags that he's dropping. Jeanine heads over to the living room sofa.

"Welcome home, little Odo. This is all yours." Faustin picks up some bags he had dropped.

Jeanine turns around. "For now."

"Yes, for now. I need to wash. Do you need anything before I do?" Faustin shuts the door.

Jeanine sits on the couch, playing with the baby. "No, I have everything I need here."

Faustin walks up the stairs.

In the bathroom, the foggy mirror displays Faustin's silhouette behind the shower glass as the constant spray of water is heard. The thick steam in the room causes a struggle to see details around. He reaches out and grabs the towel that's hanging on the hook on the wall as the water shuts off. He steps out, making a refreshing sigh and wrapping the towel around his waist.

Wiping the moisture off of the mirror to see himself better, he pulls his lip up to check his teeth. Through the mirror, he notices a shadow under the door darting by. He quickly turns around and opens the door.

"Jeanine…" He looks in the direction of where the shadow went and sees nothing.

Jeanine yells from downstairs. "Are you out of the shower yet?"

He turns to his wife's voice and then looks back in the direction of where the shadow went.

He hesitates and stutters. "I… I just finished. I'll be down in a minute."

Jeanine stands in the doorway, fidgeting and looking a little nervous with a somber-looking older man. Faustin eagerly lopes down the stairs. The older man lifts his head, and Faustin notices the pain in his eyes. Faustin's eagerness turns to hesitation, and he slows down drastically.

"What? What is it?" Faustin grows concerned.

The older man clutches his khaki newsboy cap in his hands. "It's John. He's had an accident."

By the look in the old man's eyes, Faustin already knows the truth, but he still holds on to a glimmer of hope. "What do you mean?"

"He's dead!" the old man adds.

Jeanine covers her mouth while she gasps and then slowly crouches down on the bottom step. She stares at the ground and shakes her head in disbelief. Faustin passes her as he rushes down the rest of the steps and approaches the old man.

He holds his hands out and pleads to the old man, "What happened?"

"He lost control of his car last night and ended up running head-on into a truck." The old man's eyes start to draw tears.

Shaking his head, Faustin holds his hand up to put a pause on what the old man is saying. "Wait, John has always been a cautious driver. It had to have been the other driver."

"John's car was in the other lane. The police saw that the tire marks swerved into the oncoming truck. John was at fault." The old man puts his hat back on and steps to the front door.

Faustin backs up to the bottom step and takes a seat with Jeanine. He puts his head down in his crossed arms and sobs uncontrollably. Jeanine leans over and wraps her arms around her husband, giving him some comfort.

"I don't believe that's what happened," Faustin weeps.

9
FAUSTIN

Ikoyi cemetery/John's funeral

The day fits the mood of the crowd. It's dark and gloomy, with nothing but dingy cumulonimbus clouds overhead. A large cluster of family members, friends, and well-wishers gather around the casket while the preacher preaches incoherently. Although there is no rain, some people hide below umbrellas just in case.

Hovering over the shoulders of the elderly sitting in the front row, Faustin stares blankly at the closed casket with photos of a youthful John's smiling face on it. He focuses on the Yoruban charms that have been placed on it while the preacher's voice starts to fade away. He recalls strange memories with John.

On a sunny day, an eight-year-old Faustin scampers along the tree line with an eight-year-old John. They play sword fighting with some old sticks. The sound of other children playing echoes in the distance.

"You can't battle with Ozula, the greatest warrior ever." Faustin takes a swing.

"Why do you always get to be Ozula?" John connects with Faustin's stick.

"Because I called it first. How do I know if you're Ozula if you don't say anything? You have to beat me to it," Faustin explains.

John becomes a little angry, and his aggression intensifies after Faustin says that.

Faustin cautiously blocks the powerful swings. "I'll let you have it next time for sure."

John stops swinging his sword and reaches into his shirt. He pulls out a shiny silver necklace with a slightly rusted elephant head as the charm. "I've got the power of Ozula here."

Faustin leans in to take a closer look, though not as captivated about it as John is. "That's not the power of Ozula. That's something your grandfather made."

They glance toward the faint sound of children to make sure they are still playing in the schoolyard. No one seems to be paying any attention to the two boys, so they make their escape into the dark woods.

"Come on!" Faustin hurries.

Being reluctant, John hesitates a little, then finally follows. "Where are we going?"

They dash through the woods, giggling and shouting. Slowly, the trees start to become thicker and thicker until all of them become leafless Iroko trees. The landscape seems to be more rugged and old-looking, and the crunching sound of each step that the boys take kills any thought of moisture in the area.

"You can't keep up." Faustin slows down his pace.

They stop running and start to look around. Although the trees are leafless, sunlight still struggles to break through, causing a chill in the air. There's thick bush everywhere, almost sealing itself off from the rest of the world. There's a complete, eerie silence.

They notice some old small toys—water guns, little black dolls, yo-yos, and little black plastic action figures—dangling from small tree branches. A couple of inches above the toys hangs a sign reading "Odo Okan."

"What is this place?" John curiously gazes around.

"I don't know. I've never been here before." Faustin steps closer to a tree and squints at the Odo Okan sign. "Young souls?"

John jerks his head back to look behind him. "How come we don't hear the other kids anymore? We didn't run that far."

Faustin's curiosity turns to complete astonishment by his surroundings. "I've been in the woods many times but have never seen this. Look at that."

Faustin starts to slowly walk further in, causing John to become a little nervous. "We should go back."

"Wait a minute," Faustin continues to step forward.

John becomes panicky as his nerves elevate his voice. "The others are going to wonder where we are."

Annoyed, Faustin turns to John and raises his voice. "If you want to go back, go ahead. I'll be there in a minute."

John hesitates a bit but eventually turns and runs back into the narrow opening that leads back toward the schoolyard. Faustin is left standing there only to hear the sounds of silence.

He takes a couple of steps deeper into the area and hears a child-like voice. The near-incoherent voice is so faint and almost seems smothered. "You must go!"

Faustin freezes and confusingly scans more but sees nobody. "Hello?"

He takes two more steps, and the voice becomes more coherent. "You must go!"

He stops again and takes a long and careful look around but sees nothing.

Faustin takes one more step and hears a light giggle of the voice. "You must…" The voice turns raspy and sinister. "…stay."

Faustin's awareness heightens, and he turns to head back to the narrow opening, but it's not there anymore. There's more thick bush in its place, so he looks around in a panic while, one by one, different children's muffled voices start to erupt.

He turns and darts toward where he last saw the narrow opening and explodes through the thick bush. He stumbles to the ground and quickly feels his hands sinking through the dirt as if he were being swallowed by the ground.

Giving a slight tug and pulling himself back to his feet, Faustin continues scampering back to the schoolyard. Panting heavily as he runs, he turns to look back and sees a blurry silhouette of someone standing at the edge of the narrow opening, staring at him. The children's voices become fainter as Faustin leaves them behind.

Back to the present day and out of Faustin's memory, he continues to stare at John's casket. He quietly mumbles to the casket. "You knew something was in there, didn't you, John?"

Jeanine gives him a nudge. "What? Did you say something?"

"Nothing!" Faustin's mind snaps back to the funeral.

Everyone starts to move slowly alongside the casket in a circle, taking turns tossing a handful of dirt on top of it. Faustin grabs some dirt from the ground and inches his hand forward, hesitating. He finally slings the dirt on the casket.

10
FAUSTIN

Nwaike Residence

It's a quiet night with a little somberness mixed in with it. Faustin and Jeanine lounge on the couch with the television lighting their faces.

Faustin has his eyes halfway opened and staring at the television as if caught up in the program. "Did Odo go to sleep without a fuss?"

"Peacefully."

"Good!"

Jeanine tries to initiate more conversation with Faustin. "It was a beautiful ceremony today."

Faustin gives no response and continues to stare blankly at the television.

Jeanine tries again. "You know, when John—"

"Jeanine, not now!" Faustin cuts her off.

Jeanine gives off a loud sigh. "Okay, I'm tired. I think I'll go to bed."

They give each other a little peck on the lips, and she gets up and starts to walk out.

Faustin keeps his attention on the television. "Okay! I'm not too far behind you."

"Okay!" Jeanine proceeds up the stairs.

Faustin sits there staring at the lit-up tube. There is complete blackness in the house behind him, with the exception of a small strip of dim light shooting through a window in one of the back rooms.

A shadowy figure very slowly creeps from the blackness and crosses over the dim light before slipping into another shadow.

Rubbing his eyes and feeling like he can't keep them open anymore, Faustin clicks the remote control and turns the television off. Getting to the top of the steps and stepping down the hallway, he notices the black bag that John slipped the amulet into. He picks it up and unzips the front pouch, finding the amulet inside. Trying to keep it discreet, Faustin quickly glances down the hallway toward the bedroom to make sure Jeanine isn't seeing anything. He gives a slight smirk with a little head shake before turning thoughtful.

Little Odo sleeps soundly in his baby crib when Faustin tiptoes in. He tries to be as quiet as possible by moving cautiously and reaching into the crib to attach the necklace and charm to one of the side panel bars. He then covers it with a small baby blanket and leans in to give his son a small kiss on the head.

"You will always be protected," he whispers.

Faustin exits the baby's room and leaves the door cracked before continuing down the hallway. The crack in the door sits still, and there is no other movement as the house gets brighter from the sunrise.

***

Five months later

Faustin comes walking back to the baby's room. Little Odo is standing up in the crib and bouncing up and down with morning excitement.

"What are you doing?" Faustin picks the baby up and gives him a kiss.

He takes a quick glance back toward the door before reaching down into the baby's crib and slowly pulling the baby blanket down, exposing the amulet. He quickly picks it up and shoves it into his pocket.

"Today's the big day, my son. Later tonight, you will be sleeping in America." Faustin bounces his son in his arms as he walks out of the room.

Descending the stairs and into a completely empty floor level, he hears the echoes of every step. Jeanine comes walking in from another room.

She reaches in and grabs the baby. "Have you been a good little boy?"

"Yes!" Faustin jokingly answers, knowing that she's talking about the baby.

"I wasn't talking about you." She rolls her eyes.

They turn and take one last look at the house that they have spent so long in. The feeling of excitement of going to a new place mixed with the feeling of bittersweet of leaving precious memories behind rushes through them.

Faustin sighs loudly. "This is it, the last time we'll see this place. The house I grew up in."

"You didn't grow up here," Jeanine corrects him.

"You know what I mean. We've spent many years here," Faustin corrects himself. "I look around and remember the many good times we had here."

She walks out the front door. "We'll have many good times at the new home."

Faustin spends a few more seconds mentally reminiscing. "Goodbye, John."

He walks out and slams the door shut.

11
FAUSTIN

Lagos International Airport/Departure Day

The airport sign reads, "Murtala Muhammed International Airport." Revolving doors constantly spin, cycling, hurrying travelers in and out of the building.

Inside, herds of travelers scurry along as announcements are constantly being made over the loudspeaker. Faustin and Jeanine sit patiently in the airport's steel waiting seats. Jeanine bounces the wide-eyed baby on her lap while Faustin fidgets around anxiously.

"We'll get to the house, set up everything, then I'll go to Johns Hopkins to take a look around." he nervously plans the near future.

Jeanine pauses the bouncing of the baby. "Wait a minute. As soon as we land, you will not have enough energy to do all of that."

"What do you mean?"

"I mean, as soon as we land, you will be tired. We will get to the house and sleep on whatever we can find because I guarantee you that the furniture has not arrived yet." She starts to bounce the baby again.

With his legs still nervously bouncing around, Faustin sits back in his seat and sighs deeply.

"And I hope they don't expect you at work right away," she adds.

"I can't wait to get started. I'll go to the hospital to look around and meet people. You know, break the ice a little bit." He rubs his upper thighs, feeling antsy.

"Okay," Jeanine huffs.

A black lady has a seat on the back side of the steel chairs behind Faustin. She sits perfectly and abnormally still. She goes unnoticed by all, but with a dirty brown scarf tied around her unkempt hair, the back of her head briefly catches Faustin's attention before Jeanine's voice causes him to completely disregard it.

"You know, we haven't really researched any schools for little Odo," Jeanine says.

Faustin shrugs. "What is there to research? He's not going to be in any school anytime soon."

"In the future," she says in a playful baby-like voice on Odo's face.

"Yes. We have plenty of time." Faustin notices a gate agent standing by himself and watching travelers. "I'll be right back."

"Okay!"

Faustin gets up and walks toward the agent.

"Mommy's little baby boy. Who's my little baby boy?" she says in a baby voice.

The black lady with the scarf turns her head slightly toward Jeanine and Odo, but her face is never shown. She turns only to direct her ear toward the mother and infant son.

"Daddy's a little excited, and I am too."

She puts the baby over her shoulder to reach into her bag. As she searches, she hears the continuing tiny giggles of the baby but pays it no attention.

She searches and searches, unable to find what she's looking for. "Where is it? Never mind."

She pulls the baby back to her lap while he still giggles, and she twists her face from a foul smell as she takes a whiff. "Eww boy!" She lifts him and focuses on his diaper. "No, it's not you."

She quickly glances around, her nostrils flaring from sniffing, trying to find where the smell is coming from. Faustin returns to his seat. "The man over there said we will be lining up in about ten minutes. Let's get a good place in line."

They grab their carry-on bags and start to move toward the terminal. The black lady with the scarf still doesn't move an inch in her seat.

Stepping first in the terminal line, travelers one by one start to come in from all directions and line up behind them. The gate guard makes the announcement. "Now boarding for Baltimore, Maryland."

Faustin and Jeanine wait anxiously in front of a long line of boarding passengers while the black lady with the dirty scarf stands motionless and overlooked in the back. Her face is still never seen.

12
UMAR/FRANKLIN

Roosevelt High School

In the principal's office, the principal sits behind his fancy black oakwood desk, holding a thin, opened folder of records in front of him. His eyes bounce back and forth with uncertainty from the records to Dr. Fulani and Franklin, who sit across the desk.

Dr. Fulani sits back in his chair, steady and with a strong and unwavering look in his eyes. Franklin slumps down in his seat with a slight scowl on his face. His eyes bounce back and forth from his father and the principal. Everyone sits there trying to read each other with nothing being said. The tension is so thick that the sharpest Obsidian blade couldn't slice through it. The clock on the wall ticks.

The principal hesitates but musters up enough courage to open his mouth. "To let you know, we are well aware of your son's… activities at the last high—"

"I understand that," Dr. Fulani quickly responds before he can finish.

The principal slowly closes the folder, sighing and shaking his head. He knows he's taking a big risk. "I'll tell you, Dr. Fulani, knowing his history, he will have very little chances here at Roosevelt."

"What do you mean?"

The principal elaborates. "I mean, the first time will be the last time. He will get no more chances."

Dr. Fulani nods in agreement. He's clearly upset about the lack of confidence in his son, but he completely understands and bites his tongue. Giving Franklin a good stare-down while his son looks back, he silently warns Franklin of his short chances.

The principal cuts his eyes to Franklin. "You can see Mayvis on your way out. She will get you your schedule for the year."

Dr. Fulani reaches out his hand and shakes. "Thank you, sir."

They get up, and he walks out of the office with his son to the secretary's desk. The principal stands there staring at them through the doorway, breathing deep sighs of possible regret.

Zigzagging down a crowded school hallway that's full of students dressed in their black and white school uniforms, Dr. Fulani and Franklin almost have to move sideways. There are nothing but white students with the occasional black face appearing. The father and son get several looks from curious students walking by.

Dr. Fulani seems a little annoyed, constantly dodging students while he gives Franklin a small lecture. "Judging by the looks of these students, it'll be pretty difficult for you to fall back into your old habits here."

Franklin twists his face at the students walking by him. "These students look nerdy and lame."

"Exactly. And that's good. These so-called lame students will keep you out of trouble," the doctor reiterates.

"Nothing but white students here with a few black folks. These few niggas probably ain't nothing but some corny Uncle Toms anyway." Franklin scoffs.

Dr. Fulani aggressively but subtly grabs Franklin's arm and pulls him close. "It starts today. You will end all of that today. You will definitely turn into a product of your environment. You will act like the students who are around you. If they are corny Uncle Toms, then you will be one also."

Franklin rolls his eyes at his father. "Yeah, sure."

"I got you away from those little thugs and gangsters. Maybe these students will rub off on you," Dr. Fulani continues.

Franklin notices a couple of white girls eyeing him lustfully as they walk by. He mumbles to himself. "They could definitely rub something off on me."

"What?"

"Nothing." Franklin turns his head back to walk with his father.

They stop in the middle of the hallway as kids continue to walk around them. Dr. Fulani steps close to his son's face and speaks in a low, aggressive manner. "Pull your class schedule out and follow it. I have to get to the hospital."

He walks away, rolling his eyes and shaking his head while Franklin stands there contemplating his next move. He pulls out his class schedule and takes a look at it.

In the parking lot, Dr. Fulani walks to his car and pulls out his cell phone. "Yes, he's in there. He's not too happy about it, but he'll get over it."

He opens the car door and looks up, noticing a lone black high schooler swinging on the swing set of a neighboring elementary school playground. The black high schooler stares with trance-like wide eyes without blinking. He thinks nothing of it, so the doctor continues into his car but takes a second cautionary glance at the kid through the rearview mirror before driving away.

The bell loudly rings, and Franklin hesitantly tries to creep into a classroom filled with students preoccupied with a little socializing in clusters before the start of class. He tries to go unnoticed when two male students dart past him to get in and accidentally push his shoulder. Franklin gets upset but tries to stay subtle and keep attention off of him. The classroom of students still notices and stops all of their chatter to stare at him as he stands in the doorway.

"Everyone, please have a seat," the teacher yells.

Franklin starts walking, aiming for a seat in the back. Everyone focuses on the new kid in the class, checking him up and down as he steps closer and closer to his desired seat. Franklin scans the room as he walks and when his eyes are shifting, a crumpled-up piece of paper smacks him in the head. Several students burst out in a short cackle as he aggressively turned toward the direction it came from.

The teacher acts very nonchalantly and is not surprised by the behavior, but he feels that he has to go through the motions of doing his job. "Who did that?"

There is a small group of white boys in the back corner of the class. They have a menacing look about them and snicker with the rest of the class while eyeing the new kid. One of them stands out of the crowd because he's the one kid who keeps his head aimed at his desk. He looks guilty by trying not to look guilty and gives off the vibe that he could be the leader of the group that sits around him.

Franklin slowly continues to his seat while some students giggle quietly, and one mumbles in the background, "Another monkey broke out of the cage."

Remembering his father's words, Franklin takes a seat without saying anything. With his fists balled tightly and his jawline clenched, it's obvious that he wants to react to the nasty comment.

He notices that a couple of white high school girls give him some lustful looks of interest, so his tensions ease a little, and he relaxes his fists and strains to bring a smile to his face.

Class ends, and Franklin's eyes are half open due to the boredom. The bell rings, and he snaps out of it and jumps up from his seat to the hallway. Walking casually down the hallway, his eyes are constantly watching people from the natural paranoia that's been built up from his previous school experiences. A couple of white girls approach him overzealous with big smiles on their faces.

"Hey! How are you?" One girl leans in.

"Good." Franklin stays calm and shows a little lack of interest but manages to smile a little.

The girl bounces with excitement. "This is Courtney, and I'm Megan. We are the captains of the cheer squad here at Roosevelt, and we're trying to recruit new members."

He becomes a little confused about why they approached him about cheerleading.

"We are specifically targeting cute guys, I mean, strong-looking guys, because we need more boys to fill our team for competition."

Her friend leans in and hands Franklin a slip of paper. "Here's the tryout schedule. They don't last long at all. Show up and show us what you've got."

"Sounds aight. I may have to check it out," Franklin responds with fake zeal.

The two girls walk away giggling while Franklin rolls his eyes at the invitation and continues walking down the hallway.

He spots the bathroom and heads for it. He gets within a few feet of the bathroom door, and a boy steps in his way. The boy is very eccentric with his eyeshadow on, blue-dyed hair, and gothic-style makeup. He wears a blank look on his face and is completely emotionless.

"You must be the latest exemplification of this primordial foundation." The goth has a monotone voice.

"What?" Franklin's seriously confused about the boy's perplexing vernacular.

"You're new at this school." The goth stands there, staring into Franklin's eyes.

Franklin hesitantly responds, "Yeah, I just got here today."

"We could use a new breed in class." The goth hands him a drama class and theatre flyer.

Franklin glances at the flyer. "I've had my fair share of drama at my last school. No, thank you."

Franklin hands him the flyer back and proceeds into the bathroom.

He stands in front of the urinal, relieving himself while his eyes roll back into his head. The sound of the other students in the hallway elevates and then becomes quiet again, as if someone came through the door. He slightly turns his head toward the noise for a split-second without actually looking at who came in. He finishes up and shakes before turning around.

Three white boys from his class stand there smirking. One of them casually strolls over to the sink like everything is normal. He's dressed in well-fitted slacks with a button-down collared shirt. His preppy look is completed, with his hair slicked to the side. Franklin doesn't feel any kind of a threat.

The white boy turns the water on and starts washing his hands. "Hey, Billy, my dad hired three new guys at his company."

"Oh yeah?" Another white boy stands back with his arms folded, smirking and staring dead at Franklin's eyes.

The boy by the sink continues to wash his hands. "Yeah, two white guys and some African."

When the white boy said that, Franklin freezes, a little shocked and feeling the possible problems that are arising.

"So I asked my dad, knowing that he always hires whites, why he chose to hire the African for a clothing textile factory. He told me that he's learned that nobody knows cotton better than a nigger." The white boy pulls out a paper towel and starts drying his hands.

Franklin fidgets and nods, trying very hard not to react to the comment while the other white boys stand snickering. The boy finishes drying his hands and then turns to Franklin and acts nonchalant, like nothing was said.

"Oh, hey. What's up? My name is Thomas." He arrogantly reaches out to shake hands.

Franklin doesn't try to shake and leaves Thomas's hand hanging in the air.

Thomas pulls his hand back. "No, my bad, brotha."

The other white boys continue to snicker.

"Let's get out of here." Thomas turns to his friends, and they head out laughing.

Franklin starts to rub his head and pace back and forth, trying not to explode with rage. He exhaustedly leans against the wall to take a couple of deep breaths with his head in his hands.

A strange voice raises Franklin's head. "Are you okay?" A teacher stands there with his hands on his hips.

"Yeah, everything is good." Franklin scurries out of the bathroom.

Sneakers screech on the shiny hardwood floor while teenage girls battle on both sides of the volleyball net in the gymnasium. The sound of cheering and motivating their teammates on both sides echoes throughout the open area.

"It's coming to you, Kendra." One girl bounces the ball up, giving an assist to another girl.

The second girl leaps and spikes the ball down hard while letting out a big thrusting yell. The velocity is too much for the other side of the net, and the ball bounces through them. The scoring side cheers.

The overzealous forty-year-old female coach intervenes and aggressively blows the whistle. "Now that's how you are supposed to spike it, Kendra. Show no mercy. If I ever see you do what you did last week against Augusta, you will be riding the bench for the rest of the season. Keep doing exactly what you did here."

Franklin comes cautiously, walking through a side door at the top of the bleachers and quietly has a seat. Nobody notices him, and they keep practicing.

Franklin looks in wonder with his mouth wide open at the sight of the girls in their tight and skimpy volleyball shorts. He focuses on each part of each and every girl on the court, lusting after them. "Damn! She looks good."

"Come on! Let's see more of it. I want more," the coach rages at the top of her lungs.

A girl throws the ball in the air and smacks a serve to the other side. A girl from the other side smacks it out of bounds.

"What the hell was that, Natalie?" The coach blows the whistle.

The ball comes bouncing onto the lower bleachers, and one of the girls retrieves it. She looks up and notices Franklin in the stands and gives him a flirtatious smirk. Franklin smirks back.

The coach belches out loud enough to spit. "Hey! You can't be here. Who are you?"

Franklin gets up and quickly walks back through the door that he came through.

13
FAUSTIN

En Route to America

Lounging in the comfortable aisle seat of the Boeing 787, Faustin jots in his journal while Jeanine's head rests on his shoulder, the baby snug in her lap. All is quiet on the aircraft due to most of the passengers soundly sleeping. All that is heard is the soft rumble of the engines.

He looks at his lovely wife and son with a smile, relishing the luck of having such a beautiful family. He looks around at all of the passengers and sees that everyone is at peace. He slides his journal to the side and into the seat beside his leg before sitting back, closing his eyes, and taking a deep breath of relaxation.

Faustin slowly starts to peek through his eyelids as they gradually open. He gazes around and notices everyone still sleeping. Turning and taking a look at his wife sleeping on his shoulder, he struggles to open his eyes completely. He keeps an easy smile on his face, feeling the joy of their upcoming new family life in a new land. His eyes lift and navigate toward the opened slide, exposing the window. The reflection of a black woman with deep and dark hollowed-out eyes and brown jagged teeth lingers over his shoulders, staring at him. He quickly jerks around, and she's inches from his face, staring him in the eyes.

She speaks slowly and raspy with John's voice. "O tele ni pekipeki." (She follows closely.)

He opens his eyes and jumps forward, breathing heavily from the nightmare.

Jeanine sits wide awake with the baby on her lap. "Is everything okay?"

"Yes, everything's fine." He looks around very carefully with paranoia, eyeing each and every passenger within view and eases back down to close his eyes.

Among the light traffic of travelers, Faustin briskly walks through the airport. Jeanine walks at the same pace but is clearly uncomfortable walking so fast.

"I know you're excited about your job, but remember that it's not going anywhere," she huffs from the effort.

"What do you mean?" Faustin's eyes are constantly scanning around him.

"I mean, you don't have to walk so fast. It'll still be there whenever we get there." She smiles.

"I know it'll still be there, but I can't wait to get there." He continues to look around, causing Jeanine to wonder.

"Are you sure everything is fine?" She briefly glances to her left and right, then back at him.

He becomes a little annoyed. "Yes, for the last time, everything is good."

They continue briskly walking. Jeanine rolls her eyes at his urgency.

Outside of the airport, a line of taxis awaits the travelers' money. Faustin and Jeanine approach the closest one as they exit the airport doors. The driver is a young black man in his early thirties.

"Let me take your bags and put them in the trunk." The driver reaches for the luggage.

"Thank you very much." Faustin appreciates the gesture.

The black driver hears the African accent in his voice and becomes ecstatic. "Ahhh! From the mothaland. That's what's up. Hop on in, my African brotha."

The driver shoves the bags into the full trunk and struggles to shut it. He gets in and starts rambling on before he attempts to turn the ignition.

The driver turns around. "Ah, man, that's cool, being from Africa and all. I always wanted to go there. I think every black man and woman should make it a priority in their lives to visit the mothaland."

Faustin and Jeanine look extremely annoyed but keep strained smiles on their faces.

"So, what part of Africa you from? Zimbabwe, the Congo, Burkina Faso."

"Nigeria," Faustin cuts in.

The driver's face is gleeful as he turns and starts the engine. "Oh shit! Nigerian niggas up in this bitch."

The car screeches off. On the road, the taxi driver can't get enough of conversation about Africa, as he eyes the rearview mirror. Faustin grins and bears it with overdone smiles on his face while Jeanine rolls her eyes, shakes her head, and huffs in annoyance.

The driver comfortably rambles. "Shit, I always thought African clothes were the hardest. A slick dashiki shirt with a smooth-ass kufi on top. A nigga would get all the pussy with that shit on. Excuse my language."

Jeanine doesn't pay any attention to the driver and gazes out of the window. While cruising down the highway, she sees down below the rundown project buildings with trash covering most of the streets. The homeless linger while trashy-looking prostitutes walk from car to car, propositioning. She notices a few locals on the street sleeping, standing up but slumped over like zombies.

"This is beautiful, isn't it?" Faustin giggles with excitement.

Jeanine simply turns to him, displays a fake smile and turns back around to look at the mess.

The taxi pulls up in front of a beautiful little two-bedroom home. It's quaint and cozy-looking from the outside, with freshly cut grass and flower beds left by the previous occupant lining the front. Neighborhood kids scamper by as other neighbors tend to their own yards with care.

Jeanine turns to Faustin with a real smile. "Now, this is beautiful."

Faustin hands the driver the cash for the ride while Jeanine quickly exits the car with the baby.

"Thank you, my African brotha." The driver takes the money, pops the trunk, and exits the taxi to pull the bags out.

Faustin slings a couple of bags over his shoulders and carries the rest. The driver gets back in and throws a tightly clenched fist out of the window and into the air as he pulls off. Faustin takes a moment to scan the area, enjoying the sight of the neighborhood. He feels a great sense of achievement in himself being there.

"Are you coming?" Jeanine stands at the front door of the house.

Inside the house, the emptiness draws an echo from the door cracking open. The family steps in and immediately stops to take it all in. Faustin closes his eyes and takes in a big, relaxing whiff.

"Yes, it has to be cleaned before I am comfortable." She notices Faustin smelling the air.

"I am already comfortable." He sets the bags down beside the opened door.

"I think you'd be comfortable anywhere. You'd be comfortable living in a barn." She easily walks deeper into the homes, bouncing the baby in her arms.

Faustin closes the front door and scampers from room to room with excitement, checking things out. His steps have a nonstop echo through the house while he runs upstairs. "It has two bedrooms."

Jeanine continues to walk deeper into the house, and her eyes are scanning every inch. She breathes a big sigh. "What do you think, Odo? Yeah! It'll do fine."

He comes back downstairs, stumbling a little bit from skipping several steps. With his hands on his hips and his energy drained from his body, he breathes heavily from all of the running. "What do you think?"

Jeanine smiles and nods. "I like it."

"I do, too. I think this will be fine." He wraps his arm around his family.

14
FRANKLIN

Roosevelt High School

The cafeteria is packed full of students. There is a very organized flow of traffic from the start of the entry into the cafeteria to when the student is finished eating and leaving.

Franklin slides his way down the food assembly line, picking out what he wants. He turns away from the line and scans the entire area, looking for an open seat as he slowly walks. From a distance, he spots two open seats and heads toward them. When he's within a couple of feet, two white guys come from nowhere and take the seats. They never give Franklin a second look. He shakes his head and starts looking for more seats, so he starts walking.

The next table over has an empty seat, and Franklin speeds up to try to get to it. He gets to within a few steps of the seat, and another white guy quickly slides in and snatches it. The boy doesn't even look at Franklin either. Feeling a little suspicious that this is all a setup, Franklin looks around and notices a group of white guys laughing at him.

Franklin's eyes focus on one particular person in the group, which is Thomas, who seems to be leading. Franklin has figured that he has had enough.

"Hey!" He taps the white student on the shoulder.

The boy looks up at him and answers with a smirk. "Can I help you with something?"

"Yeah, you can help me with something by moving your ass from my seat. I was going to sit there." Franklin asserts himself.

"Wouldn't you be more comfortable somewhere else? These are white-only seats." He arrogantly smirks.

Franklin snickers, hiding the anger that's building inside of him. "White-only seat. That's funny."

The white kid nods toward the far side. "You should be sitting over there with your people. The cool people. The down people. You dig… homeboy?"

Franklin looks to the far side of the cafeteria and notices all of the black students sitting together. It's an area close to the bathroom and is not considered to be a desirable area to eat.

Franklin gently sits his tray on the table and tightens his fists. The principal steps in and distracts the two boys with a couple of quick grunts, clearing his throat. He picks his tray back up and proceeds to the area where the rest of the black students are. He turns while walking and gives a mean mug to the groups of boys led by Thomas.

Later in the school day, the school bell rings, and all classroom doors swing open in the hallway. A sea of students quickly flood the center, scampering to freedom. Franklin walks alone, zigzagging through thick traffic and through the exit doors. He stops when he gets outside and takes a deep breath while the blurs of students scurry past him. He notices his father's vehicle parked and waiting, so he hesitates to proceed.

"You shouldn't let them do that to you." A strange voice comes from close to him.

He looks to the side and sees a teenage girl posted in the corner and lighting a cigarette. Her skin is ghostly pale white with black eye shadow and thick black lipstick. Purple and blue strands flow through her deep brunette hair, and tiny shiny silver hoop rings pierce through each alar cartilage on both outer nostrils.

"Whatchu talking about?" Franklin tries to cover his nose while being subtle about it.

"I was watching you in the cafeteria today. Those boys do that to every black kid who shows up here. The more you let them have, the more they'll take." She keeps a calm demeanor.

He tries to keep his distance from the smoke. "I ain't trippin' over it. It's not a big deal."

The girl scoffs and snickers. "Yeah, right. I saw how mad you were. You get pissed off like that, but it's not a big deal? I'd hate to see when it is a big deal."

Getting upset, he turns his head away, trying not to say the wrong thing.

She takes a puff of her cigarette. "I don't know why people are so afraid to stand up to Thomas and his friends. They are a bunch of damn dorks if you ask me."

Franklin quickly turns back around, snapping at her. "Who the hell said I was afraid?"

She snickers. "Well, shit. You let them run over you, didn't you? You let them force you into the, quote-unquote, back of the bus section. By the way, that's what everyone calls that area."

"The only reason I didn't bust his shit is because of that man right there." He points to his father's vehicle.

The girl looks over at the fancy Audi Prestige and squints. "Who is that?"

"My father. I promised him that I wouldn't fuck up here like I did at my last school," he explains.

"Suit yourself." She takes a long drag and then tosses the rest to the grass.

Franklin scoffs, then turns and walks away. She yells toward him. "I'm Raven."

He never says anything or looks back and hops into the car. Dr. Fulani sits, staring in Raven's direction.

"Who's that you were talking to?" he asks before Franklin could even shut the door.

Franklin shrugs. "I don't know. I came outside, and she started talking to me out of nowhere. I've never seen her before."

Dr. Fulani stares at his son for a few seconds before shaking his head, starting the car and pulling off.

15
RAVEN

Raven's home

Doom metal blares in a bedroom that's lit with red lights. There are red sheets draped over the lamps and scattered small candles lit throughout the room. There are dolls hanging from black shoe strings in random places and black-painted skulls posted on the hand-carved black enchantment dresser. The bookshelf is stocked with Aleister Crowley's work mixed in with the work of Anton Lavey. A pentagram covers the center of the hardwood bedroom floor.

Raven stands in front of her dresser dressed in her black, see-through gothic Widow Maxi Dress with a black bra and panties. On her feet are Demonia Metal Militia boots. With a glazed stare, she studies herself in the mirror that's posted on top. Lying flat in front of the mirror is a photo of an old woman and a younger Raven in happier days.

She closes her eyes and starts chanting in a low whispering tone as if she's trying to contact the dead. She pulls out a black and silver crusader cross spring-assisted pocket knife from her upper right-hand drawer and unfolds it. She slices across the top of her index finger and drips drops of blood all over the photo.

She whispers to herself. "Contented days are no more, Grandma."

After the last drop of blood onto the photo, she hesitates a little, letting the blood drip from her finger to the floor while staring at the blood-soaked photo. Another dresser drawer is jerked open, and Raven pulls out a box of bandages and tissue paper to wrap it.

Downstairs in the living room, a man in his mid-forties kicks back in a reclining chair with a bottle of beer in his hand. He has a couple of buttons on his plaid shirt unbuttoned, showing his beer belly poking through. His blue jeans are covered with dust and dried paint, and he's basking in the air of his flatulence. The big flat-screen television has a home renovation show playing that the man's eyes are glued to.

"You asshole. You have to sand that shit down first," he mumbles to the television.

Raven comes down the stairs. Her boots loudly knock on the hardwood, causing the chandelier to noticeably vibrate.

The man's eyes pull away from the television. "What the hell?"

She enters the room wearing the same thing as she was wearing during her ritual.

"You need to be that damn loud to come downstairs?" he complains.

She heads over to the bookshelf but rolls her eyes at the man while en route.

He studies her outfit. "I guess you were upstairs doing some of your weird shit again."

She shuffles through some books on the shelf, and he slowly scans her up and down, lusting. His hand slides down to his groin as he slowly rubs and squeezes. She quickly turns and catches him in the action. Putting on a lustful smirk, she strolls over to him and leans into his face, displaying some cleavage.

"You like what you see?" she flirts.

She places each of her hands on each of his knees and slowly slides her hands up, going toward his crotch.

"Are you sure you'd know what to do with me, Hank?" she asks.

Hank sits back and enjoys the moment. "Well, stepdaddy knows best."

"You like little sixteen-year-old girls? Forbidden fruit always seems more tempting, huh?" She rubs his legs closer and closer to his crotch.

He snickers. "Age ain't nothing but a number, baby."

She grabs one of his arms by the wrist and slowly rubs it up her body and to her breast, circling the breast as he feels. His mouth is wide open as he enjoys this statutory moment.

"You like that?" she teases.

"Yeah, but I'd like it even better if you let me get up inside you."

She quickly shoves his hand back to his beer belly. "Yeah, right. You wish you could feel something like this, you old perv."

She goes back to searching the bookshelf, leaving Hank to himself. He takes a big swig of his bottle of beer and quickly fixates his eyes back on the television when a woman in her mid-forties enters the room. The woman sags everywhere and stays in a nightgown with rollers in her hair. She walks with a cloud of smoke covering her from the cigarettes that she carries and looks as though she couldn't care less about being a mother.

"Hey, girl." She passes by Raven.

Raven snatches a book from the shelf and turns to walk away. "Hey, Donna."

Heading to the sofa, Donna turns with the cigarette in her mouth. "I guess the word 'mom' is too much, huh?"

Raven never turns back around and keeps walking up the stairs. Donna yells at her, "Keep dressing like that; the whole town'll wanna fuck ya like a little whore, if they don't already."

Donna takes a seat and slams her slipper-covered feet on the tables.

Hank pretends to act somewhat like a guardian. "I tried to tell her—"

Donna cuts him off quickly. "Shut up. I know for sure you wanna slide your dick inside her. Turn the TV onto my stories."

He stares at her for a couple of seconds before picking the remote control up and clicking it to another channel.

In Raven's room, she has it darker than before. The lampshades are covered with dark red sheets. Lit candles line the outer edge of the pentagram, while the book that she retrieved downstairs sits wide open in the middle.

She covers her face with a black veil as she steps into the center of the pentagram carrying another lit candle in a brass taper candle holder. Dropping to both of her knees, she places the lit candle to the side and picks up the book. The whispers of her chanting start very faintly and gradually grow into a moderate tone, but still incoherently. The language is not of English but of sorcery. The moderate tone grows louder, as if she's trying to reach something or someone.

There's a slight creak of the door, and her eyes open widely. She looks toward the door and sees it cracked open with her mother's face peeking through, smothered by the cigarette smoke.

"Can you keep that shit down, please? I can't even hear the damn television." She blows cigarette smoke.

Raven rolls her eyes. "Yes, Mother. Whatever you wish."

Donna slams the door shut, and Raven continues with her chanting, but at a lower tone. She substitutes the noise elevation with rapidness and motors through her words, repeating the same things over and over with sharp emphasis. Her words start to echo around her as she gets deeper into focus.

All of a sudden, she stops and opens her eyes. There's nothing but silence around her.

16
FAUSTIN

The New Life

Many months have passed by, and Jeanine washes dishes in the kitchen sink. All is quiet in the house except for the clinging of the dishes when, all of a sudden, little Odo comes running around the corner, laughing and giggling. He stumbles a little because he's not fully coordinated with his legs yet.

Jeanine notices and turns around with a smile but continues to wash dishes. "What are you doing, Odo?"

The baby babbles and cackles loudly at the sight of his mother.

"I'm sorry I can't play with you right now." She smiles at him.

Faustin comes into the room dressed in slacks and a button-down shirt with a tie. On his face, he has new glasses. He gives Jeanine a peck on the cheek, grabs a coffee mug from the dish drain, and then grabs the hot coffee pot and pours.

"Sleep well last night?" She turns and asks while continuing with the dishes.

"Yes, of course. Way better than usual." He takes a sip.

"You really seemed like you did. I woke up a few times and looked over at you, and you were snoring loudly." She snickers.

"Yeah, I tried everything from the sleep disorder center at the hospital… and nothing. Simply go to the pharmacy store and buy some of the gel caps… and I sleep like a baby."

Jeanine looks down at her son. "Not even Odo sleeps the way you did last night."

He continues to sip his coffee, enjoying the peaceful moment, looking at his family. The baby walks up to his father and starts waving with a big morning smile.

"Hey, little buddy." He sits his coffee cup on the counter and bends down to pick his son up. Little Odo strains to reach for Faustin's new eyewear, and Faustin leans back and giggles.

"I heard back from Roosevelt yesterday. I can start as soon as next week."

Faustin is overcome with joy and a sense of relief. He gives Jeanine a kiss on the back of the head.

"That means we have to find someone to watch Odo." She turns around and leans against the sink, folding her arms. Her smiles turn to seriousness.

Faustin takes her by the hand for a measure of comfort. "Don't worry. We'll find someone we can trust."

She gives a relieving nod and turns back around to finish the dishes.

"I have to get to work now," He slides Odo down his body, turns to take one last sip of his coffee, then gives Jeanine another peck on the cheek and heads for the door.

Faustin slowly pulls into the parking lot of the medical center, avoiding medical staff who pass by. He parks the car and exits, walking casually toward the employee entrance, flipping his keys in his hands. In the blurry background, another employee exits his vehicle and starts to walk in the same direction. The closer Faustin gets to the door, the closer and clearer the other employee gets to him. It's Dr. Umar Fulani arriving at work and unrecognizable by Faustin. They give each other a nod before entering the entrance doors together and parting ways when they get in.

Dr. Fulani fades further and further into the background while Faustin proceeds, walking through the doors of the occupied waiting room.

The receptionist quickly pokes her head from around the corner, causing Faustin to jump. She is a young white girl with perkiness running all through her. She keeps a low whisper when she speaks. "Ms. Marshall has been waiting for you."

Faustin drops his head and gives a slight shake. He hands the receptionist his jacket and other personal belongings. "Can you put these away for me?"

He enters the examination room that's almost entirely paper-covered. Dieffenbachia plants posts in each corner of the room, creating a warm and cozy vibe. A white lady in her seventies sits in the examination chair, slightly swinging her legs. She looks frail but in good spirits, and her skin hangs from her body.

Faustin washes his hands thoroughly in the office sink. "Ms. Marshall, glad to see you."

"You are?" She lifts her head.

He dries his hand with paper towels he pulls from the wall and straps on blue latex gloves. "Well, maybe not in these circumstances. But I'm glad to see you."

He gently slumps her over and slides the magnifying lamp over her shoulder before pulling the back of her shirt down, revealing a pink fist-sized rash. He examines it very closely. "It looks a little better. Less redness… Blistering has gone down drastically. Is it still itching?"

She shakes her head.

He pulls her shirt back up. "I'm going to reduce the antibiotics a little more. We will schedule you to return in exactly a week, and you should be all cleared up."

She turns and gives a smile.

They exit the examination room, and he puts his hand on Ms. Marshall's back to nudge her along. The receptionist sits at her desk, typing information into the computer while another patient stands in front of her. Faustin refers Ms. Marshall to the receptionist.

He leans into the receptionist and whispers, "I'll see her again in about a week."

"Okay, I'll take care of it," the receptionist answers, turning her head but not taking her eyes from the computer.

He checks his watch, proceeds back into his office and closes the door. A fluffy black carpet covers the hardwood of his office floor. There's a plushy two-seater sofa with a stool against the back wall directly across the room from his office desk. ZZ plants are in the corners of the office. It feels like a cozy living room with an office desk in it.

He slides one of his desk drawers out and starts shuffling through different patients' files. He thoroughly studies each and every file that he comes across. There's a knock on the door.

"Yes?" He doesn't take his eyes off the files.

The door pops open, and a female assistant leans in. "What time do you want the meeting to be?"

"Tell everyone to be there in about fifteen minutes." He checks his watch.

The assistant nods and shuts the door. He continues to study files and mumbles to himself. "Ms. Marshall is coming in another week. Mr. Avery and Ms. Chaney should be here today."

He shuffles through more files, slightly nodding his head and coming to some conclusion. "It should be a pretty good day today."

Later that night, at the new Nwaike residence, Faustin pulls into the driveway. A young lady who looks to be in her early twenties walks down the porch steps waving while Jeanine stands in the doorway waving back. She notices Faustin pulling in and getting out of the car, so she stands there waiting for him.

"Who was that?" He ascends the porch steps while watching the young girl get into her car.

"She's a babysitter." She continues to block the doorway as they stand there, watching the girl drive away.

"That's the babysitter?" Faustin responds with surprise.

"No, that is not the babysitter. That is a babysitter. She's only one of many I'm interviewing."

Faustin nods and then turns to her, staring at her, blocking the doorway. They look at each other for a good three seconds before

Faustin says, "Is there something wrong with me getting into my house?"

"Is there something wrong with me getting my kiss?" she counters.

He snickers and leans in to kiss her. She moves to the side, and he walks in.

Inside the house, he slings his jacket on the coat rack beside the door that she's shutting. Little Odo runs around like crazy, making plenty of noise, and the aroma in the air causes Faustin's nose to flare with sniffs.

"Something smells good." He starts to walk toward the kitchen area.

"Dinner will be ready in a little bit."

He stops at the countertop and calmly searches through a thick pile of mail while she continues to the stove and starts stirring the pot of stew that she's been preparing. Little Odo runs through the kitchen as if he's charged up on sugar, and Faustin giggles while dodging the wild child.

"You said that the girl was only one of many. How many have you interviewed today?"

Jeanine pauses, stirring the pot and squints in deep thought. "There were about… nineteen or twenty."

Faustin's eyes widen and roll back down to the stack of mail that he holds.

"All of them are young girls, though," she adds.

Faustin looks at her and shrugs as to ask the problem with the age.

She turns and notices his reaction. "What? Young girls are very immature. They'll be having to watch Odo and then end up having some boyfriend coming over here…"

Faustin shakes his head with a slight snicker.

"There'll be more tomorrow." She turns back around to tend to the pot.

Faustin drops the stack of mail back on the countertop, turns and walks down the hallway and up the stairs. Jeanine yells to him, "There's a fresh towel and washcloth folded already for you."

The full body spray beats down while Faustin enjoys his shower. Thick and cloudy fog, almost as thick as the Grand Banks of Newfoundland, causes the surroundings to be barely noticeable. Condensation from the steam covers the mirror and walls. With nobody anywhere near the mirror, the moisture slowly rolls down the mirror, causing a clear view. Faustin stays oblivious and continues to shower.

Later that night, all is quiet as everyone is sound asleep in their beds. Little Odo sprawls out in his little crib, and Faustin lies on his back with Jeanine lying halfway on top of him with her head on his chest and arm slung across. There's a continuous slow drip from the bathroom sink with the faint sound of chirping crickets leaking through the closed bedroom window. Nothing out of the ordinary is visible, but the feeling of eeriness lingers in the dark house as if something or someone silently creeps around. Faustin cracks his eyes open, exhaustingly scans the room, and falls back to sleep.

The morning has arrived, and Faustin sits at the kitchen table, eating his scrambled eggs and reading the newspaper. Little Odo sits in his chair, struggling to hold the spoon to eat his cereal while Jeanine prepares a place at the table for herself. She sits and starts to enjoy her breakfast, and there's not a single word said for a while until it's time for Faustin to leave.

He folds up his morning newspaper and polishes off his breakfast plate before taking it to the sink to place it in. "You have more interviews today?"

"I assume so. Nothing scheduled, but whoever shows up will be interviewed." Jeanine rises out of her seat and follows her husband toward the front door.

Faustin gives his wife a peck on the lips and slings his jacket on. He opens the door and leaves while she stands in the doorway waving goodbye. She slowly scans the cool outside and crosses her arms to shield herself from the chilled breeze before shutting the door.

17
JEANINE

Nwaike Residence

Jeanine continues back toward the kitchen and sits down to finish her breakfast. Odo still struggles to hold the spoon to finish his breakfast. Jeanine giggles and grabs the spoon out of his hands to get a scoop of his cereal and place it in front of his mouth. He leans in and bites, putting on a huge smile of happiness for his mother.

After breakfast, she gets up and pulls Odo from his seat and to the floor. He immediately takes off, darting toward the living room rambunctiously.

"I'll be in there in a minute to turn on the television for you." She places her plate in the sink.

Walking toward the living room, Jeanine stays oblivious to much of her surroundings as she aims her sights solely on what's directly in front of her. She rounds the corner from the kitchen to the living room, and the back door displays a silhouette of someone standing there on the other side of the shade. Little Odo sits on the floor with his toys scattered around him as she clicks the television onto some cartoons. She walks back toward the kitchen, and the silhouette of the person has vanished.

Jeanine proceeds to run some dishwater and gather the remaining dishes from the table and countertop. The dish bubbles slowly climb on top of one another, and the steam rises to her face. She smells the soothing steam and closes her eyes, taking advantage of the very little time to relax on that day.

There's a knock at the front door. Jeanine cracks the door to where only half of her face is shown, and a young girl about sixteen years of age stands there with a confusing smile. She has a backpack on as if she's on her way to school.

"Yes?"

The girl looks back and forth at the house number and Jeanine. "I might have the wrong house, but is this where the babysitting job is?"

Jeanine swings the door open with the biggest smile on her face. "Yes, it is."

In the kitchen, Jeanine sits the young girl down and offers her a beverage. "Would you like something to drink?"

The girl pulls out a manilla folder from her backpack and opens it, showing some paperwork. "No, thank you."

Jeanine slides the paperwork toward her and skims through it. She nods impressively as she goes down each page.

"It looks like you've been pretty busy, Jessica," Jeanine stresses the credentials.

"Yeah, I do pretty much most of the babysitting in this area. Me and another girl."

Jeanine jokingly snickers. "There's no kind of serious competition between the two of you, is there?"

"Not really. She got upset a couple of times and said that I took a job from her."

Odo comes running into the kitchen while the two are talking. He stops and stares at Jessica with wide eyes, trying to figure out who she is. She leans in, talking to him in a baby voice. He cuts his eyes over to his mother and points to Jessica, asking who she is.

"Are you in school or anything?" Jeanine closes the girl's folder and slides it back to her.

The girl grabs the folder and shoves it back into her backpack. "I'm on my way there now. I figured I'd stop here first. You know… get the jump on it."

"Ah! Before the other girl catches wind of the job." Jeanine smiles, causing the other girl to giggle.

"I suffer from a pulmonary condition. I've been approved for some medical leave from school for three weeks. So I'll be able to be here easily. After the three weeks, we can work some other things out." She straps the backpack back on.

They both rise out of their seats and proceed toward the front door.

"I start my new job next week. Can you be here around 7:00?" Jeanine opens the front door.

"I will. And I'll stop by tomorrow, too."

They both say their goodbyes, and Jeanine closes the door.

In the kitchen, Jeanine puts her hands into the dishwater and starts to scrub when she freezes, realizing that she needs something else. She dries off her hand with the dish towel that's slung over the sink and opens the cabinet above. Moving things around, she's unable to find what she's looking for, so she searches other cabinets around. She finds no success with her search and stands there contemplating.

"Odo, we have to go to the store to get some things." She places a couple more dishes into the water to soak while they're gone.

The supermarket is dead, with only a few people in the massive store. Jeanine slowly pushes the grocery cart down the aisle, checking out everything that the store has to offer. Little Odo sits in the baby seat of the grocery cart.

She stops to look at some green scratch pads and tosses them into the cart along with a new bottle of dishwashing liquid. Continuing down the aisle, she constantly scans from left to right, carefully eyeing everything in sight and making sure that she doesn't pass anything that she needs.

Odo notices something a few feet behind his mother. It's a black woman in her late forties with unkempt hair that's tied in a ponytail with a dirty brown scarf. She slightly slumps forward behind her cart and makes baby noises for Odo's attention. Jeanine doesn't notice due to something on the shelf catching her attention. Odo gives off a small giggle at the strange woman.

"What are you giggling at, boy?" Jeanine doesn't take her attention off of the shelf.

Odo intensifies his giggling, and Jeanine pulls her eyes away from the stock. "What are you…" Her words are cut short when she turns and notices the strange woman.

The woman freezes and then straightens up to Jeanine. She moves from behind her cart in a peculiarly rapid fashion and sticks out her hand to shake. Jumping back slightly, Jeanine stays a little cautious about the woman but manages to keep a smile on her face to shake hands.

"I'm Charlena. I didn't scare you, did I?"

Jeanine hesitates to speak. "No… no, you didn't scare me. I was a little surprised, that's all."

Jeanine squints at Charlena, going into thought. "Have we met before?"

"I don't think so."

Charlena leans in and gently tickles the baby in the seat. Little Odo starts giggling at first but then takes a detailed gaze into her eyes, seeing what's really behind the eyes of the strange woman. He looks up at his mother with a pouty face and tears forming in his eyes. Noticing that Odo is uncomfortable, Jeanine intervenes.

"Well, it's nice to meet you." Jeanine tries to rush the conversation to an end.

Charlena's head pops up from the baby. "What's your rush?"

To Jeanine, she gives off the vibe of a crazed and homeless woman who could be very desperate. Jeanine cautiously tries to keep the situation calm, not really knowing the mentality of the woman.

"Well, I have a lot of things to do around the house. I only came out to get a few things to finish cleaning." Jeanine slowly starts to walk away, pushing the cart along.

Charlena sticks to Jeanine's every step. "You seem like you're very busy. Maybe you need someone to watch the boy while you work."

Jeanine speeds up her walk, trying to create distance between her and Charlena. "No, thank you. I already have a babysitter."

Charlena slows down in her tracks and comes to a complete halt. She continues to watch Jeanine and Odo with a menacing smile on her face as they rush through the checkout counter. Jeanine suspiciously glances back a couple of times.

Outside in the parking lot with only a handful of cars, Jeanine finishes placing her groceries in the trunk of the car while Odo sits in his back seat car seat. She closes the trunk, hops into her car, and pulls off. She slowly cruises to the parking lot exit when Odo catches her attention with some babbling.

"I know… That was strange for me, too." She adjusts the radio.

She moves her hand up to adjust the rearview mirror and freezes, noticing the strange woman standing outside of the grocery store focused on their car driving away. She stands awkwardly, hunched over as if she's zooming in on the car.

Jeanine sits there for a couple of minutes at the edge of the parking lot exit, watching Charlena. Nothing on Charlena's body moves even an inch the entire time Jeanine is watching her. It's almost like she's frozen in some trance state or possessed.

Shaking it off, Jeanine proceeds forward and out of the parking lot.

18
FRANKLIN

Roosevelt High School

The classroom is all quiet, with the exception of a few snickers here and there from a group of boys in the back corner. There are a couple of paper airplanes floating across the room as the students sit in silence, preparing for the start of class. Franklin slumps down in his seat, doodling on a pad of paper. He's not too eager to crack a book open.

The middle-aged male teacher walks in and sets his briefcase down next to his chair. The students become more erect in their seats while he turns and picks up a small piece of chalk and starts scratching letters across the board. Franklin silently huffs and rolls his eyes, dragging his book out and opening it.

The teacher turns to the class and prepares to open his mouth when he's quickly interrupted by the door opening. In walks a sixteen-year-old black kid who no one has ever seen before.

"Yes, can I help you?" the teacher asks the boy.

He hands over a slip of paper to the teacher.

"Oh, okay. Grab a seat, and we were about to start today's lesson." The teacher points to an empty chair in the front corner of the room.

The boy slides in his chair, and the teacher begins to spit out the lesson, which fades away in Franklin's ear due to his interest in the new kid. Maybe it's the fact he's only one of two black kids in the class, but the fascination with the new kid is unknown to Franklin. He subtly leans out of his seat to take a look, but all he sees is the back of the head. The new guy keeps looking straight ahead and doesn't turn his head enough for Franklin to catch a good enough view of him.

All of a sudden, the teacher's words shoot back into Franklin's ear. "Is there something wrong, Franklin?"

Franklin jumps back into his seat and shakes his head.

At the end of class, the bell rings. Everyone scurries to pack their things into their backpacks and out of the room. Franklin keeps his eyes on the new boy while he shoves his own books into his backpack. The new boy starts to head out into the hallway, and Franklin tries to keep up with him, struggling to zip up his pack.

Into the hallway, Franklin darts out of the classroom. He scans from left to right, trying to find the new boy in the thick herd of students. He finally spots the back of his head and follows at a distance, trying to be subtle. The new boy walks through the hallway without speaking to anyone, as if he knows his way around already. Passing students greet Franklin as he follows. He quickly speaks back without taking his eyes off of the new boy. Rolling his eyes like something's bothering him, Franklin quickly notices the restroom door and contemplates going in.

"Fuck it!" He cuts to the restroom and eyes the new boy, who continues to walk away as he enters the door.

"Draining the lizard" in the urinal, there is a calming silence, with the exception of a faint sound of the students passing by on the other side of the restroom door. The sound of the students never elevates as the door seemingly stays shut. Franklin shakes, zips, and turns around to find the new boy standing there. Franklin jumps back. "Oh shit!"

The new boy speaks with an African accent. "I'm sorry. I didn't mean to frighten you."

He slides by Franklin to the urinal, and Franklin stands back, watching him while he urinates. All of Franklin's toughness and coolness are pushed aside. He has a fascination with this kid for some reason. He can't put his finger on it, but it's as if the new boy has some secret strength that Franklin senses from him.

The new boy finishes up his business at the urinal and starts to wash his hands. Franklin continues to stare at him, standing in the same spot.

"I like this school. It is beautiful like a rose." The new boy doesn't even look up from the sink. "I haven't met many people here so far, but it seems like a good place."

"Huh! Give it some time," Franklin scoffs.

The new boy snatches some paper towels and turns to Franklin while drying his hands. "What do you mean?"

"I mean that this place is just like a rose. It may seem good in the beginning, but once you get a little too close, it starts to smell like shit."

Franklin bursts out in a loud cackle, and the new boy gazes at him confusingly.

"That's not a nice thing to say, Franklin."

Franklin's cackle comes to a quick end when he hears his name. "How the hell do you know my name?"

The new kid holds his hands out toward Franklin. "That's what the teacher called you in class, right?"

Franklin goes into thought, trying to remember the time in the classroom that his name was called.

"Oh yeah, right," He reaches out to shake the new boy's hand.

The new kid quickly pulls his hands back and cautiously stares at the greeting hand. Franklin's wide eyes jump back and forth from his hand and the boy, trying to figure out why he doesn't want to shake his hand.

Without saying a word, the new kid steps to the side, giving Franklin a clear view of the sink. Franklin comes to the realization that he hasn't washed his hands yet.

"Right." He rushes over to the sink to wash and then dry.

He sticks out his hand to the new boy again and finally gets a hand in return.

"Lukozi." The new boy shakes back and speaks extremely politely, with a smile frozen on his face.

The two immediately connect with one another, seeing that they both have African heritage.

"Where are you from?" Franklin feels a connection with the new boy.

"I'm from Nigeria."

Somewhat impressed, Franklin's eyebrows rose. "My folks are from Nigeria, too. They came here when I was really little."

"What part?" Lukozi leans in for clarity.

Franklin shrugs as if he doesn't know. "What about you?

Lukozi politely chuckles. "I'm from the area of Okan."

"Okan?"

"Yes, it's a very small area of Nigeria." Lukozi holds up his index finger and thumb about an inch apart from each other. "We've come here for a short time, and then we're going back.

"You and your family?" Franklin meddles.

"Me and—" Lukozi's words are abruptly interrupted by a group of young boys bursting through the door.

Thomas and his crew enter, cackling loudly and joking with each other when they notice the two African boys standing in the middle of the restroom floor talking.

"Howdy, boys! We didn't interrupt your gay African fuck scene in here, did we?" Thomas rudely comments, making his friends cackle louder.

Franklin rolls his eyes. Without being introduced to Thomas's immaturity and bullying yet, Lukozi confusingly looks back and forth from Franklin to Thomas.

The rowdy white boys walk past the African boys and gather over by the opened window. A pack of cigarettes appears from the pocket of one of Thomas's followers, and they each grab one stick.

"I'm Lukozi." He approaches the white boys with a smile on his face.

Thomas takes a drag of his cigarette. "You're also a nigger. Get the fuck out of my face."

Not knowing the foul vernacular of the typical rebelling American teenager, Lokozi stays oblivious to what is said to him and keeps a smile on his face.

"That will kill you." Lukozi points to the cigarette.

Thomas gives him a serious gaze of aggression. "What are you, my mother? Get the hell away from me, boy."

Franklin gently taps Lukozi on the shoulder as he kindly smiles and waves goodbye to the white boys.

Exiting the restroom and back into the crowded hallway, the two African boys follow the flow of traffic.

"Whose class do you have next?" Franklin dodges around fellow students, trying to keep up with Lukozi.

"Actually, I don't have class right now. I have to go somewhere." Lukozi seems to be a little preoccupied with something other than school rushes ahead of Franklin, leaving him stopping in his tracks.

"Okay, I'll catch up with you later," he yells past the moving crowd to the distancing Lukozi, who never looks back to give a response.

19
FAUSTIN/JEANINE

Nwaike Residence

Later in the evening, Faustin walks into the front door of the dimly lit house. The only light on, the kitchen light, bounces off of the walls, giving a little illumination to the surrounding rooms. He notices no one and closes the door. He stands at the door with his eyes squinting around in complete silence, trying to hear any sound of occupancy or see any kind of movement of shadows from around a corner.

"Jeanine?" With a low tone, he cautiously cries out for his wife's presence.

He walks into the kitchen and doesn't see anyone or any dinner being prepared. He circles back around to the living room and stands there in the shadows for a split second, still trying to hear some movement in the house. He walks to the edge of the staircase and looks up before slowly starting to ascend the steps.

Upstairs, he notices the same thing as downstairs. No movement at all and blackness, only to be lit by the moon shooting through one of the upstairs curtains opened. He stands in awe, trying to figure out what to make of it.

"Jeanine?" His panic mode slowly starts to set in as he belts out his wife's name and rushes downstairs. He nervously searches every room and jerks back every door to open them.

Breathing profusely, he finally stops in the kitchen and notices a side door. He opens it, and light explodes into the dark kitchen. He looks downstairs and yells. "Jeanine?"

Jeanine's muffled voice responds to her husband's desperation. "I'm down here."

He descends the basement stairs, with every step creaking to the point of almost breaking, to find Jeanine pulling clothes out of the dryer. The loud washer is continuous with a smooth rumble that causes an elevation in speaking between the two. Little Odo sits on a blanket that's sprawled out on the hard cement floor, playing with some old toys.

She lifts the laundry basket full of dried clothes and notices Faustin's sweaty face. "Are you okay?"

He gives her a kiss and goes over to his son to give him a kiss. "Everything's good."

She starts picking through the clothes. "I'm sorry dinner isn't made. I've been so busy today. I figured we could order something in."

He leans against the wall beside her. "Sounds good to me."

He takes a short moment while he catches his breath from the panicky search. She picks clothes out of the laundry basket and starts to neatly fold them.

"Did you ever find a babysitter for Odo?"

She brings a brightened smile to her face. "Actually, yes. Her name is Jessica, and she is the sweetest girl."

Faustin interrupts her, "But can she be trusted?"

Jeanine shrugs. "I trust her.

He starts picking through the laundry basket and pulling out some clothes to help her fold them. Jeanine's eyes trail into thought as if she's trying to remember something.

"I ran into this weird woman at the store today," she thinks deeply.

"Yeah?"

"She was kind of creepy and was following me around the store, trying to talk to me."

Faustin's attention stays mostly on the clothes and doesn't get too worried about what Jeanine is saying. But he is perplexed by the story.

"Following you? Maybe she liked you."

They both jokingly snicker while balling the clothes up and dropping them into the basket. She picks the basket up and starts to carry it toward the stairs. Faustin calls for Odo.

She starts climbing the stairs. "I think she was more interested in Odo."

Picking Odo up, he starts climbing the stairs, too. "Well, he's a baby. People like babies."

Entering the kitchen, she clicks the bright light on and sets the basket of clothes on the kitchen table. "This baby didn't like her."

He slides Odo down his body, and the little one runs into the living room. Faustin yells to him, "I'll be in there to turn the television on in a little bit."

He slowly approaches the back of his wife and slides his arms around her to hold her. She turns her head, and they share a few kisses.

Jeanine gives her husband a love tap on the cheek. "The girl will stop by here tomorrow if you want to meet her and go to work a little later."

Faustin smiles and snickers with a little pat on Jeanine's backside. He walks into the living room and clicks the television on for Odo.

Jeanine slides out of a kitchen drawer and pulls a restaurant menu out from a thick stack of menus. She pulls out her cell phone from her pocket and dials. "I'd like to place an order."

The morning has come, and Faustin is all ready for work. He lingers around the kitchen, constantly glancing at his watch and looking a little impatient. Jeanine walks into the kitchen and heads straight over to the already-made dishwater.

He leans against the edge of the counter. "When is this new babysitter coming? I have to get to work."

Jeanine gives a big sigh. "Then go to work. You'll see her another day."

Faustin quickly steps over to his wife and gives her a kiss on the cheek. She smiles and dries off her hands with the dish towel before walking him to the front door.

The door opens, and he steps out. "See you when I get home."

She smiles and waves as she stands in the doorway. Faustin's car can be heard revving up and pulling off while she scans the outside, searching for any sign of Jessica. She gives up and shuts the door.

Two weeks have gone by, and there has been no sign of Jessica. Faustin sits at the breakfast table while Odo is eating. Jeanine comes walking into the kitchen dressed for work in her back-to-school dress for comfort and style and her hair in a bun. She grabs a cup of coffee and looks a little fidgety.

"She hasn't called or anything?" Faustin looks up at her and shovels down his cereal.

Jeanine shakes her head. Faustin looks back down to his bowl, shaking his head. "Not a good way to start a new job."

Jeanine constantly glances toward the front of the house, searching for anyone approaching the front door. "If she doesn't arrive and we can't find anyone else, I can't go today either."

Faustin continues to talk, trying to scarf down his food. "It's not a big deal if you want to take more time away from work. We'll find someone else."

She stands against the counter, sipping on her hot cup of coffee, contemplating. She slowly breathes the steam in to soothe her nerves. There is some comforting silence for a couple of minutes before she places the cup on the countertop and scampers into the living room. She takes a long and detailed gaze out of the front door window and sees nobody.

"You might as well call the school now and delay your start." Faustin's shoes clack against the hard wooden floor as he walks into the living room.

She continues to scan out of the door window before taking a quick glance back to Faustin. "Yes, I know."

Two seconds haven't even passed before she takes her eyes off of the window upon hearing the doorbell ring. Shocked, Jeanine jumps back and turns back around to the window. Faustin calmly steps in front and opens the door slowly, displaying Charlena's face from the grocery store. She's a little better put together this time, with her face glowing with cleanliness and a smile, an African-print twisted-braid turban on her head and a beautiful stoned Ankara Boubou gown draping her body.

Faustin stands with a huge welcoming grin on his face while Jeanine is frozen in awe at the sight of the woman.

"Hello. Can we help you?" Faustin greets her.

"Yes, I was looking for the babysitting position that was available."

Faustin's widened eyes dart back and forth from a frozen Jeanine and Charlena. He mumbles to Jeanine, "Looks like you can attend day one of work now."

Jeanine lifts her hand toward the front porch. "Where were you?"

She's cut off by a very eager Faustin. "Yes, the position is still open."

Jeanine quickly cuts in, trying to stop her husband from hiring the woman. "It's been filled."

Faustin turns to Jeanine and explains the situation to her. He speaks very low, trying not to let Charlena hear him. The other babysitter hasn't arrived yet. We need someone to watch Odo while you work."

Jeanine sighed and studied Charlena, trying to quickly find out what type of person she really was. Faustin waits for a response from his wife.

Jeanine musters a fake smile. "Welcome to our home. Come in."

The couple moves to the side and opens the door a little wider to let Charlena in, but she doesn't budge from that spot. She stands there with a strange smile on her face. Faustin and Jeanine slowly glance at each other in confusion.

"Everything okay?" Faustin asks Charlena.

She nods.

"You can come in if you…" Charlena moves swiftly through the doorway before Faustin could finish. The couple stands there, stunned at the woman's awkwardness.

She slowly scans the house, checking out every inch in detail while Faustin and Jeanine close the front door. Charlena quietly and discreetly starts to smell the air in front of her as if she's smelling for food. The couple doesn't notice because all they can see is the back of her head.

"I'm Faustin, and this is my wife, Jeanine."

She answers quickly and then completely disregards the introduction, as if she's more interested in the house.

"I'm Charlena. You have a nice home."

"Thank you." He eagerly rubs his hands together.

Charlena jerks around to face them with a big smile on her face. Faustin stares back with the same while Jeanine, feeling a little apprehensive, stands with seriousness on her face and her arms folded.

"Have you done this type of work before?" Faustin leans forward with his hands out to her.

"Yes…" Charlena stops speaking when she notices a smell in the air. The smell is something enjoyable to her, and her eyes grow almost twice the size as normal as she turns back around to the living area, where Odo quietly walks from behind the sofa with a toy in his hands.

"This is our son, Odo." Faustin stands in the blurry background. "He's the one you'll be watching."

Charlena slowly crouches down to greet the little one. His young eyes look at her and then look at his parents. Charlena reaches in, pulls Odo in and gives him a big, soft hug.

"What do you have there?" she says to the young boy in a baby voice while eyeing the toy in his hands. He stares at her blankly, not knowing what to feel about the situation.

"I see you are from Africa as well. What part?" Faustin asks.

She keeps her head aimed at Odo, but her eyes slide to the side, speaking to Faustin behind her. "I'm from Okan, Nigeria."

Faustin is overcome with confusion and looks at Jeanine with bewilderment. "Okan? I don't know where that is.

Charlena stays crouched around Odo while talking to Faustin. "It's very small. That's where I've done most of my work."

Without thinking any further, Faustin shrugs off the fact of not knowing where that place is and feels an instant connection with Charlena, being from the same country. He stands in the same spot, twisting and turning his body as he points toward different areas of the house to let the new babysitter know how to navigate around. Jeanine never says a word but studies Charlena closely.

Faustin wraps up his tour of the house for Charlena and feels comfortable enough to leave her with the baby. He opens the front door and starts to step outside when he notices Jeanine still watching the babysitter closely.

"Jeanine!" He waves her toward the door.

She stutters cautiously before hesitantly walking through the doorway, with Faustin nudging her along and shutting the door.

Walking to the car, Faustin hands her the car keys. "Don't forget to pick me up on your way home."

They hop in the car and pull off.

In the house, Charlena watches the car leave through the window and then turns to find Odo standing there staring at her. She slowly creeps closer to him as his eyes raise higher toward her, and he takes a couple of steps back.

In the car, Faustin rambles about what he has to do for the day at work. He talks about the meetings that he has and the patients who should be coming in. Jeanine stays perfectly silent as Faustin explains his day plan.

In the house, Charlena pulls a black bottle from a bag that she carried in and damps her fingers with the clear, oily substance that's inside of it. Smearing the liquid across Odo's forehead, he follows Charlena's fingers with his eyes, not knowing exactly what is happening.

In the passenger seat of the car, Faustin continues to ramble on about his day, staying oblivious to Jeanine's demeanor. She becomes a little antsy and starts to shake her head and grip the steering wheel tightly. She slams on the brakes and jerks the steering wheel all the way to the left until the car is aimed in the opposite direction. The tires screech, and traffic honking in anger while Faustin calls for Jeanine in panic.

"Wait! What are you doing?" Faustin panics while gripping the dashboard for security.

The car revs down the street and slides to a screeching halt in front of the house. Huffing and heaving, Jeanine scrambles out of the car and up the walkway, bursting in the door.

Charlena sits on the sofa and leans down to the floor to wipe Odo's face off with a baby wipe. Jeanine pants heavily as she stops to observe.

Charlena looks up. "Did you forget something?"

Jeanine is frozen, not knowing what to say and trying to hide her concerns about the situation, so she mutters out, "I… I forgot something upstairs."

She turns and heads upstairs while Faustin waits at the front door, talking to her in a low tone. "Is everything okay, Jeanine?"

Faustin closes the front door and walks upstairs after her. A sinister smirk slowly comes to Charlena's face because she knows why Jeanine rushed back to the house. Half of the black bottle of liquid pokes out from under the sofa, and Charlena rushes to try to hide it. Her foot gently pushes the bottle farther under the sofa and out of view.

Upstairs, Jeanine frantically paces around the bedroom when Faustin enters. He opens his mouth as if he's about to speak, but his wife cuts him off.

"I don't like this at all. We need to find a new babysitter."

Trying to be discreet, Faustin quickly closes the bedroom door to a small crack and starts talking in an elevated whisper. "What are you talking about? We've found one."

Jeanine stops pacing and stands with her arms folded while wiggling her leg back and forth at the knee joint from restlessness. "I don't know, but there's something about that woman that is not good. I saw that in the market that one day."

Faustin squints his eyes from confusion. "Wait, you've seen her before?"

"Yes."

They both stand there for a few seconds, contemplating with uncertainty.

"I'm not going to work today."

Faustin shrugs, pretending not to care. "Okay, then you'll probably be fired. Not showing up on the first day."

"There'll be other jobs."

He lets out a big sigh and turns to open the bedroom door.

Tiptoeing down the stairs without making a sound, the couple tries to take a glance at Charlena before approaching her. They slowly poke their heads around the corner of the stairway wall and notice Odo playing with his toys on the floor, but there's no sign of Charlena.

"Is everything okay?" A quick and sharp blurt comes from below the stairway wall. Charlena stands within feet, staring at the couple.

They finish descending the stairs normally without creeping quietly. Jeanine walks straight over to Odo and picks him up.

"Everything is fine. She's feeling a little sick today and decided not to go to work."

Charlena doesn't have a reaction but freezes, expressionless.

"We're sorry. We won't be needing you today." Faustin humbly opens the front door.

Charlena hesitates for a second and then walks over to grab her bag. Jeanine watches Charlena closely while Odo is bouncing in her arms.

"Maybe next time she will feel better." Faustin lets Charlena out through the front door. She doesn't say a word as she leaves.

He shuts the door and looks at Jeanine with his arms out.

"What!" She continues to bounce the baby in her arms.

Faustin rolls his eyes and opens the front door again. "I'm going to work."

20
FRANKLIN

Roosevelt High School

A crowded cafeteria that's filled with students enjoying their lunch break is being used with an easy and controlled flow of traffic. Franklin is lounging and enjoying his meal in the section with all black kids. His headphones are on, and he bobs his head up and down to the tunes that he listens to while occasionally glancing up and scanning around the cafeteria. The audio of Franklin's surroundings is completely cut off from him. He seems not to be bothered anymore by the segregation of races while picking at his food.

"Motha fuckas ain't shit, and niggas die," he mumbles the lyrics of his music to himself.

His eyes pop up for another quick glance around, and he notices, from across the room, Lukozi carrying his tray to a seat in the section that is, supposedly, reserved for certain students. He takes his headphones off of one of his ears and lifts his head to try to grab his new friend's attention. The roaring sound of the different students in the cafeteria floods Franklin's ears in a rush.

Lukozi tracks are halted by one of Thomas's friends when he places his lunch tray on a table. There's some very understandable confusion from Lukozi as he glares at Thomas's friend and shrugs. Franklin watches as the white kid points in the direction of where he is seated. Without hesitation, Lukozi proceeds to follow the informal rules of the student population, and Franklin watches him walk toward him with his head down.

Franklin catches his attention by slightly lifting his hand and waving him down.

"Don't even worry about that. It's nothing." He waves them off like a fart in the wind as Lukozi sits down in front of him.

Lukozi doesn't say a word as he sits down and doesn't seem to be bothered by the situation. In fact, he's even cheerful as he unrolls his fork from his small napkin and starts eating.

Franklin freezes with shock, noticing Lukozi throwing one food item on top of the other. He shovels the green beans and corn in with the lasagna and mixes it up. Then he scoops the dried-up chocolate cake in with it, pours a couple of small pours of the fruit juice, and mixes further.

Franklin can't believe his eyes and is disgusted by the sight. He calmly places his own fork on his tray, telling himself that he's finished eating.

Lukozi leans down to his tray and starts filling his mouth with the weird mix of food as if he hasn't eaten in days. He never chews and smears the food over his lips and chin as if he has never been taught how to eat.

Feeling a little embarrassed for his friend, Franklin constantly glances around the room, trying to make sure nobody else is seeing what he's seeing. He squirms a little bit and discreetly holds his hands up, trying to conceal the abnormal way of eating.

Later in the day, they walk down the school hallway with a slight urgency in their step. Franklin leads the way, and Lukozi follows with confusion.

"Where are we going?" Lukozi clumsily dodges traffic from students going the same way.

Eager to get to his destination and without glancing behind him, Franklin unknowingly increases the distance between him and Lukozi, who struggles to navigate through, bumping into everyone who walks close to him.

Franklin approaches an unmarked door and turns to speak to Lukozi, who he'd expected to be there with him. He freezes, seeing Lukozi having to fight through the sea of students to finally catch up with him.

"You'll love this."

Franklin inches the door open very slowly, and they creep into the darkness.

The girls' high school volleyball team practices hard in the gym. The sound of shoes squeaking on the shiny hardwood floor echoes throughout the gym. The whistle of the coach blowing at every wrong step that a team member makes creates a chaotic scene.

The side door at the top of the bleachers slowly opens, and Franklin sticks his head through the crack to look around. "Everything's cool."

Both of the boys tiptoe in and quietly have a seat in the top corner of the bleachers.

Franklin leans into Lukozi. "I always sneak in here at the end of the day when they are starting practice. We won't be seen as easily if we sit here."

Franklin's eyes zoom in on some of the girls as they bounce around on the floor. "Look at that ass in those tight shorts."

Franklin's face is lit up with delight, and he seems to be really enjoying the show. He looks over to Lukozi and sees the focus on his face as if his mind is elsewhere.

"You okay?" Franklin nudges Lukozi, trying to snap him out of whatever he's thinking about.

He nods his head but continues to look at the girls with a serious face on. Franklin just studies him and wonders because he's never seen a boy his age who's not interested in girls.

"You do like girls, don't you?"

Lukozi never answers and stays with his head aimed at the girls. Franklin turns back to take one last look at the volleyball players. "Let's be out then, man."

Crouching down while getting up, they quietly sneak back through the door that they came in through.

They continue to walk down the hallway but at a much slower and more casual pace than before. Franklin tries to brush off the fact that his new friend might not be interested in girls.

"So what is it like where you're from?" Franklin adjusts his backpack from putting it back on.

Lukozi shrugs at the question and gives the vibe that he doesn't even want to talk about his homeland. Feeling a little annoyed, Franklin rolls his eyes and bites his bottom lip.

They exit the school doors to the outside and move to the side for the other students passing by.

"You still thinking about that lunchroom shit? I wouldn't even worry about it." Throwing away the bad cafeteria memory, Franklin swats the air.

A somewhat familiar voice comes in from the side. "I told him not to let those boys walk all over him. They will continue thinking they own the school."

Raven sits in her usual spot after school, smoking and relieving her stress from school. Franklin points at her, trying to remember her name. "Raven, right?"

She smiles and blows a puff into the air as they walk over to her.

Franklin introduces Lukozi to Raven. "This is Lukozi. Lukozi, this is Raven. You can find her out here every day with that cigarette in her mouth."

"That will kill you," Lukozi says, reminding Raven of the dangers of smoking.

Raven takes a good look at her cigarette and starts snickering before reaching out to shake hands.

Dr. Fulani pulls up on the side of the street in his car and honks his horn, getting Franklin's attention.

"Shit, I gotta go. See you guys later."

Franklin walks away, and Lukozi and Raven continue to talk, getting to know each other.

In the car, Dr. Fulani strains to see something in Franklin's direction. He seems to be frozen in awe.

The door pops open, and Franklin hops in. "What's up Pop?" He quickly noticed his father's focused attention on where he was standing with his friends.

"Are you okay?" Franklin waves in front of his father's face.

Dr. Fulani's eyes blink quickly as he shakes his head, bringing his mind back to the car. "Yes… yes. Everything is fine."

The car pulls off with the doctor taking one last glance.

In the car, the doctor's cell phone vibrates from a message while it sits in the cupholder. He picks it up and takes a look while driving. "I'm going to drop you off and then head back to work."

"Okay!" Franklin nods.

Dr. Fulani's eyes stay focused on the road, but there is a feeling that there is something behind his eyes that's disturbing him.

21
UMAR

Johns Hopkins Hospital

In the operating room at Johns Hopkins Hospital, the patient lies on his side and in the fetal position with sterile drapes carefully placed on his lower back. It's the typical hidden nervousness in the air from the staff, but not so hidden from the patient with the fidgeting.

A nurse tries to comfort the patient while keeping her own nervousness discreet. "It's going to be okay. Doctor Fulani has done many spinal taps before. You're in good hands."

The door eases open, and the doctor walks in wearing his blue hospital gown with blue sterile gloves. He sits on the stool and rolls himself toward the patient's lower back before pulling the rollable tray full of medical utensils close.

Grabbing a thin, hollow needle from the tray, he examines it briefly before aiming and slowly moving it toward the skin. As he goes into deep thought, his eyes slowly drift a couple of inches off of the target spot, and his hands start to tremble. His mind is completely away from the dangerous task that he's performing, but his hand continues to move forward and within inches of the spinal canal.

"Are you okay, Doctor?" The nurse notices his trembling hands.

He blinks and snaps out of his lost mindset, bringing him back to reality. He quickly pulls back from his patient to try to gather himself and pants as he tries to shake off any bad nerves that he might have. The patient stays oblivious to what's going on behind him.

Unable to gather his bearings, he throws the needle back onto the tray, gets up, and rushes out of the door.

"Doctor… Dr. Fulani?"

The Fulani house is dimly lit throughout the house at night. Dr. Fulani comes walking in the front door. He's met with Josephine, rounding the corner, picking up some things around the house.

"Hey!" She gives her husband a kiss on the way to another room.

"Where's Franklin?"

She yells from the other room, "He's upstairs in his room."

He hangs his jacket on the coat rack and drops his briefcase on the floor beside the door before continuing to a pitch-black room. He lingers in the doorway of the room, being cautious of the whereabouts of his wife.

The light clicks on, and his home office is nothing fancy. It's decorated with an old pinewood desk and a burgundy vinyl chair. Both of them look like they will crumble apart with one touch. There are piled-up boxes against the back wall.

He quickly and silently closes the door to a small crack and rushes over to the boxes. He shuffles through each of them until he comes to a particular one and freezes. Pulling out a vintage photo album, he gently wipes it off with his hand as he walks over to sit at his desk.

Taking one last cautionary glance at the cracked door, he cracks open the album. He flips and flips through pages of very old photos of his youth. In one, he's a baby in his parents' arms, and in another, he is a tween with his siblings huddled up in front of their Lagos home. He flips one more time, and his eyes grow while his breath takes a short break. The outer edge of the photo is jagged and shredded as if it were ripped, but it's unknown exactly what he's looking at.

22
FAUSTIN/JEANINE

Nwaike Residence

The crickets of the quiet night chirp as Faustin's car rumbles into the driveway, covering the silence of the night. The car shuts off, and he exits, looking tired and worn out from the day's work.

In the house, Odo sits on the floor playing with his toys while Jeanine folds clothes on the dining room table. The door swings open, and Faustin walks in.

"Hey!" he wheezes.

Without saying another word, he gives his wife a peck on the lips and flops down on the sofa, rubbing his eyes and letting out long sighs.

"The day was that bad, huh?" Jeanine looks at him and snickers.

"Yes, you have no idea. It was nonstop all day."

The cartoons that are on television are cut to a breaking news report. It catches the couple's attention as Faustin's eyebrows raise, but he's too exhausted to move anything else. Jeanine slightly slows her pace, folding the laundry while focusing on the breaking news.

The reporter is posted in front of an abandoned alley, reporting that a dismembered body has been found of a teenage girl. All of the limbs have been removed, and even the head. The identity of the girl is not known yet, but they know it's a teenage girl. The television reporter reports the body has been taken by the coroner, and the identification of the victim will be released later.

Faustin and Jeanine are completely in awe of the report. Jeanine takes a pause from folding the laundry and places a crumpled-up shirt back into the laundry basket to move closer to the television. Faustin strains and struggles to lift his upper body off of the back of the sofa to lean forward as the news report continues.

Recognizing a familiar spot at the scene of the crime, he squints for a better look. "I know that place. I drive by there sometimes.

Completely unaware of what's going on on the screen, little Odo constantly glances back and forth between his parents and the television.

Jeanine shakes off the shock of the television news and tries to bring some good news. "I'll be starting at Roosevelt tomorrow."

Faustin turns around in surprise.

"I interviewed another woman today. She seems sweet, especially after the last one."

Faustin becomes somewhat ecstatic and rubs Odo on top of the head. "You see that, little buddy? You'll have a babysitter, after all."

She pulls the crumpled-up shirt back out and continues to fold the laundry. "She'll be here tomorrow around the same time."

Grunting and struggling, Faustin slowly pulls himself up off of the couch, gives his son a kiss on top of the head, and walks toward the stairs. "I'm going to take a quick shower."

The bright morning comes, and the doorbell rings as Faustin energetically descends the stairs in his work clothes and opens the front door. An elderly white lady stands at the door with the biggest smile on her face. Her movements are shaky, and she speaks with a voice so soft that Faustin has to lean in to hear her clearly.

"Hello! I'm Hazel."

Not knowing why the lady is there, Faustin stands in the way of her getting inside the house. "Hello, Hazel. Can I help you with something?"

"I'm supposed to start work today."

Faustin displays a look of confusion on his face as Jeanine bounces down the stairs behind him in her black business blazer office suit with dress pants and speaks to Hazel in a soft and caring voice. "Nice to see you again, Hazel."

Faustin glances back and forth between the two of them and then is nudged out of the way by his wife. Jeanine opens the front door wider and welcomes the old lady into their home. Hazel cautiously walks with every step, dodging everything not nailed to the ground and oftentimes reaching for the wall for stabilization.

Jeanine introduces Hazel to her husband while reminding Faustin about the earlier-mentioned babysitter. "Hazel, this is my husband, Faustin. This is Hazel… the babysitter I told you about last night."

Remembering last night's conversation, Faustin nods, straightens his tie and pats his outfit, smoothing out the small wrinkles to look presentable for the new babysitter.

Odo walks up to Hazel, holding his little sippy cup and gazes at her with a blank face.

"This must be little Otto?" Hazel reaches down with her shaking hand and pats Odo on the top of the head.

"Odo!" Faustin kindly corrects her.

Jeanine anxiously but gently takes Hazel by the arm and proceeds to another room. "Well, let me quickly show you around."

Faustin leans down to his son and speaks to him in a low tone. "She seems sweet, huh? I think you're in good hands this time."

He starts to adjust and straighten his son's clothes and noticed that Odo's bottom lip sticks out, making a sad face. Faustin starts to softly wipe down his sad face with his hand, trying to make him smile.

"It's going to be okay, buddy. I know you don't know her, but I have a good feeling about this one."

Jeanine and Hazel walk back into the room, and Jeanine gives the last of the house information. "And upstairs are the bedrooms. There is enough money in the jar on the kitchen counter in case you have to go to the store for anything."

Faustin stands back up from kneeling down to Odo and links back up with his wife. They walk toward the door, and Faustin gives Hazel a gentle goodbye rub on the back.

"We'll be back at around 4:00." They exit the door.

Walking to the car, Jeanine seems to be in a completely different mood than she was when she left her son with Charlena. She had made a complete 180-degree turn and was gleeful about the new babysitter.

"I'll drive this time." Faustin grabs the key out of her hand. "I don't want a repeat of what happened last time."

They get into the car and pull away.

23
JEANINE

Roosevelt High School

Walking down the crowded hallway of the high school, Jeanine finds herself being glanced at by every student who walks by her. She has a nervous feeling of a "new kid" and hears some young male students making sexual comments from afar but manages to keep a smile on her face as she hunts for the main office.

In the main office, the secretary's cluttered desk is also well organized with stacks of papers as she punches away on the computer keyboard. The principal walks out of his office and starts shuffling through one of the many stacks of papers behind her. He tries to be discreet about it and not let the secretary know that he's searching for something.

"It's in the next one over." The secretary doesn't break away from her computer while she tends to the needs of the principal.

Feeling that he no longer has to silently move, he starts to shuffle through the next stack without the stillness that he possessed before.

He pulls out a sheet of paper from the stack and starts to walk back into his office as Jeanine opens the door and walks in. The principal turns back to see who it is. There's a short freeze of silence and confusion while everyone tries to figure out who she is.

"Can we help you?"

Jeanine grins pleasantly at the two. "I'm Jeanine Nwaike."

The secretary is overcome with surprise as she jumps up out of her chair and starts shuffling through a small stack of papers. She speaks with an overdone gleeful sound to Jeanine. "Oh! You're filling in for Mr. Robinson."

The principal finally recognizes the reason that she's here and nods with relief.

The secretary continues going down an imaginary list of the things that Jeanine has to do as she hands her a slip of paper. "You're looking for room 112, which is at the end of the hall as you make a right. When you get there, don't be too concerned with how the kids act because they always act weird."

Jeanine listens and smiles while nodding at everything she says.

"I'm sure Mr. Robinson left some kind of assignment, so all you have to do is sit there while they complete it. An easy day."

The principal never says a word, just stands in the doorway, gawking at Jeanine. She occasionally glances over to him while she receives her instructions.

"Well, have a very pleasant day, and remember, we are right here if you need help with anything." The secretary speaks to Jeanine as if she's never been around kids before.

Jeanine leaves the room and closes the door behind her. The principal finally opens his mouth. "I like her."

The secretary sits back down at her computer and restarts typing. She speaks to the principal, perkiness in her voice but a hint of boldness. "How would you know that you like her? You stood there staring at her like a creep."

Without saying a word, he walks back into his office.

In classroom 112, the class seems to already have several students in it. They talk amongst themselves in small clusters throughout the room while some still trickle in.

Feeling a little nervous, Jeanine inches her way through the doorway cautiously. A couple of rowdy boys rush by her, causing her to jump to the side.

She pulls out her rolling chair, and the students abruptly stop the conversation amongst themselves and turn their attention toward the front of the room. Jeanine is frozen and doesn't know how to react to all eyes being on her. She struggles to allow words to come out of her mouth in a room where one can hear crickets.

"Mr. Robinson should have left an assignment somewhere up there. He usually does that," one young girl speaks up.

Jeanine searches the neatly organized desk and slides each drawer open, searching for anything that would help keep the students busy for the day. She notices a clipboard in the top drawer and pulls it out.

"Okay! Here's something." She pulls the clipboard from the drawer, sifts through the papers, and carefully examines the contents. "Looks like a roster."

She slowly starts to read off the names on the roster. "Benjamin Johnson…"

"Here!"

"Sheryl Conners…"

"Here!"

"Sidney Shavers…"

"Thomas Redding…"

There is no answer from Thomas.

"Thomas Redding?"

Everyone looks toward Thomas's seat and sees only an empty chair. A voice speaks from the back of the class. "I don't think he's here today. He's the only one not here."

Jeanine marks a check beside Thomas's name and flips the paper over to move on to the next sheet.

"Since everyone else is here, your teacher left an assignment to read chapter seven and prepare for the exam that is coming up."

There are a few moans and groans as the students pull out their books and crack them open. Jeanine's relieved at the eyes being taken off of her and has a seat.

Through the students, one set of eyes catches her attention and causes her to take a double take. Lukozi blankly gazes at her with non-blinking eyes for a couple of seconds longer than everyone else before dropping his head down to his book. She shakes off the awkwardness and has a seat to crack open a book that she brought from home.

Later in the day, the bell rings, and one by one, the class slides out of the door. Jeanine waits at the door as each student passes and gives them a personal goodbye wave with a smile. They wave back the same way.

Lukozi walks past, and Jeanine gives him the same smile and wave that she gave the other students, but he keeps a stony face and doesn't even look in her direction. It's as if his mind is off into another world. Her smile slowly fades away after he passes, but she manages to slightly pull it back for the other students passing behind him.

The day ends as she rips a sheet of paper from a personal notebook and puts everything else of hers back into her bag. She jots small notes on the sheet of paper for the teacher's return and places them in the middle of the desk before exiting the door, closing it behind her.

Several students linger in the hallways, chitchatting at their lockers and gathering their things to go home. She's leaving almost as fast as the students are leaving.

A few more students wave and give a friendly goodbye to her as she continues down the hallway. She runs into a fellow female teacher rushing out of a neighboring classroom and is a little startled.

"Hey!" The teacher understandably looks at Jeanine as if she's never seen her before.

The teacher fidgets around and seems antsy about something. Jeanine braves a grin while looking her up and down, wondering what is wrong with her.

"You must be new. I'm Donna Dixon. This is my algebra class. Nice to have you here. Gotta go to the bathroom."

She dashes away and into the restroom without Jeanine getting a single word in. Jeanine stands there giggling and shaking her head.

Before continuing to walk down the hallway, she glances around, and something catches her eye behind her. From about ten yards away, Lukozi gazes intensely at her with one eye. Half of his face is shown, while the other half is behind his locker door. She quickly turns and walks in the opposite direction and takes another safety glance back, only to see that he has vanished. She slows her pace down but continues moving forward and eventually turns back around to face the direction in which she is walking.

24
FAUSTIN/JEANINE

Nwaike Residence

The car cruises into the driveway, and the engine shuts off. All that is heard are the chirping sounds of the nearby birds. Faustin and Jeanine want to take a moment to shake off the day's adventures and worries before journeying back into their house.

Inside the car, Jeanine finishes rambling on about how some of her day flashed by while another portion of it seemed to never end. "So I sat there and waited and waited. It was almost never-ending at that point."

Faustin sits back and listens relaxingly while his wife verbally relieves her stress.

"But it wasn't all bad. I met some good people. Some strange people also."

Faustin snickers

She clutches her bag to prepare to exit the car. "Young American boys are very different from the boys I grew up with."

They both exit the car and shut the doors when Faustin becomes a little curious about the young boys at her school. "What do you mean?"

She slings her bag over her shoulder as she rounds the car corner. "Some of them have this crazy stare when they look at you."

Inside the house, little Odo walks around the corner from the kitchen to the living room as the door swings open. Faustin and

Jeanine step in and shut the door behind them.

Faustin tries to put Jeanine's worries to rest. "Maybe the young boys think they like you."

"I hope not because the look this one boy gave me was a stalker look."

Faustin cackles and leans down to his approaching son to pick him up.

"Hey, buddy!" He gives his son a kiss.

They both look toward the back of the house and glance up the stairs.

"Where's the babysitter?" Jeanine sits her bag on the sofa.

"That's a good question. Hazel!" Faustin puts his son down and yells for the babysitter.

He cautiously climbs the stairs, calling her name with every three or four steps that he takes. He searches the bathroom, and the only sound and movement in there is the water smacking the porcelain sink from the faucet dripping.

He looks over toward the bedroom and sees a shadow moving on the floor from something in front of the bedroom window. He slowly tiptoes to the bedroom doorway and pokes his head in to see the curtains waving in front of the partially opened window. He quickly closes it.

Downstairs in the living room, Jeanine bounces the baby in her arms as Faustin descends the stairs and walks into the dining room. The glass back door is slid open about six inches. He opens it and pokes his head out to scan the backyard. He sees nothing but a peaceful green yard. He shuts the door.

"Where is she?"

Not knowing anything, Faustin shrugs in confusion.

"She might have left." Jeanine sits Odo down and walks over to Faustin.

"I don't know. You interviewed her."

"Yeah?"

"Well, she's a little old. She didn't seem like she wanders off or anything to you?"

Jeanine shakes her head. "She seemed to be perfectly normal." She starts to walk away. "Can you watch the baby? I'm going to take a shower."

Faustin starts to follow her through the kitchen and passes by the basement door. He freezes and backtracks in his steps. The basement door is cracked open about an inch, and he slowly opens it to see the light on and hear the dryer rumbling.

"Hazel!" he cautiously calls her name.

He starts to walk down the stairs, taking a step every two seconds. The wooden stairs sound like they are about to crack in half with every step.

He doesn't even get all the way to the bottom before he finally sees feet dangling three feet off of the ground. With widened eyes and panicky pants, he rushes down the stairs to get the full scene of Hazel hanging.

His heart almost pounds out of his chest at one hundred and twenty beats per minute, and the sound of the dryer is no more, even though he sees it still on. His senses are clogged by the fear and panic of what he sees until he hears his wife's screams on the steps.

25
FRANKLIN

Roosevelt High School

Franklin casually walks down the hallway of the school. A couple of guys say, "What's up" and give him some dap as they walk by him. A drawn-out observation of other students while he walks, lets him know there's something wrong today. There's a strange energy in the air because many of the students seem morbidly curious and even excited about something.

"Oh my God! They found pieces of him there." One of the students is heard talking low to another student.

Entering the classroom, Franklin sees the same from the students who are already seated. They talk amongst themselves with a strange excitement as he makes his way to his seat.

"What's going on?" He leans toward another male student and whispers.

The male student is very jittery and anxious. "Man, they found Thomas's body. Well, some of his body. He had been torn apart, like some wild animal got to him or something."

Franklin is frozen as he listens to the gruesome details of Thomas's death.

"We don't have anything around here that can do damage like that. His face was ripped completely off, and his stomach was wide open with his guts torn out." The boy squirms even more before turning back toward the front.

Franklin sits and stares over at the empty seat that was once Thomas's. Around the empty desk, his friends sit at their desks somberly and quietly.

The teacher walks into the classroom and sets his briefcase on top of the desk. Little by little, the students start to calm down while the teacher waits behind his desk.

"I'm sure everyone's heard the news by now. I can tell by how everyone is talking. We've lost one of our students. Thomas Redding. They're not sure of the cause of death, but they're looking at it as a very horrifying accident." The teacher speaks with a somber tone and shaky voice.

Franklin sits at his desk, not as affected by the news as everyone else is. He always saw Thomas as a snobby little racist rich kid who thought he could have his way with everything. He's shocked about the manner in which he died but couldn't care less about the person who died.

The teacher tries to ease some of the students' worries. "There'll be grieving counselors on hand for anyone who needs them."

Taking a huge sigh, Franklin sits back in his seat and pulls his book from his backpack to his desk to prepare for the day's lesson. He shakes his head slightly, shaking off the big news of today.

In the cafeteria, Franklin slides through the lunch line, picking out his sandwich, his sides, and a piece of fruit. He finally gets to the front of the line and turns around to see the same type of environment that the lunchroom has always had. Everyone is acting no differently than the day before. He can't tell if anyone's speaking about the death of

Thomas because everyone's voices are blending in as one big continuous roar.

One quick glance to the middle of the cafeteria, Franklin notices Lukozi sitting in the "white section." He devours his slice of pizza as if it's the best-tasting thing in the world at the moment, and nobody seems to be bothering him.

Franklin makes his way over to him. "What's up, man?"

Lukozi seems thrilled to see his friend and sucks the remnants of food from his fingers. "Hey, my friend. Sit with me."

Franklin hesitantly lowers himself to the next seat while gazing around for a reaction from someone. There's no reaction from anyone, and he quickly relaxes.

"You decided to make a change today?" Franklin has a little bit of skepticism in his voice, being cautious of why he chose this day to make the change.

Lukozi wipes his hands with the napkin while pushing down his food. "I enjoy sitting over there with everyone else. I heard the news this morning and thought I could sit here today."

Franklin doesn't say anything but only nods while taking a bite.

"Those guys followed the guy, Thomas, and did what he told them. I saw that when I arrived here. He's not here anymore, and look at everything now," Lukozi explains.

Franklin keeps his face toward his food as his eyes cut toward Lukozi's direction. He feels uneasy, as if Lukozi is, somehow, responsible for Thomas's demise, but has some doubt in his mind due to the severity and gruesomeness of the death. He doesn't give any indication that he's having these thoughts and keeps acting as if everything's normal.

Leisurely walking down the hallway after filling their stomachs with food, the two boys definitely don't look like they're in any kind of a hurry. Their pace is like that of a person taking a stroll in the park on a day off while students around them scurry around.

"Yo, did you see that substitute yesterday?" Franklin turns to Lukozi.

Lukozi has no response and even looks a little confused. "What do you mean?"

"The one that was subbing for Robinson. She had a fat ass on her."

Lukozi keeps a look of confusion on his face and doesn't say a word. He seems not to be familiar with the way young American boys think and feel.

"She looked sexy as hell to me," Franklin adds.

Lukozi finally realizes the person who's being spoken of. "I think I know who you're talking about. She was not fat."

"She was fat in all the right places." Franklin snickers as Lukozi continues with his confusion.

Franklin rolls his eyes and shakes his head in disbelief that Lukozi has no interest in girls. The walk through the hallway becomes quiet and uncomfortable as the boys feel at odds about teen sex life, so Franklin decides to change the subject.

"So what's it like over in Africa anyway? I mean, I've seen movies about Africa and heard my father talk about it a little, but I have never been there."

Lukozi shrugs as if African culture and customs are only a vague memory to him. "The place I came here from is very small. There's not very much to say about it. I can't remember much before that."

"You can't remember much before that," Franklin mumbles to himself.

They continue to walk in awkward silence until Lukozi bewilderedly looks around, sensing something in the air. He stops in his tracks, causing Franklin to wonder what's going on with him.

"What's up, man?" Franklin turns around to him.

"I think I forgot something. I have to go."

"You always gotta go," Franklin snickers.

"I will talk to you later."

Lukozi turns around and starts walking in the opposite direction. As he gets further away, he's obscured by surrounding students until he's completely swallowed by the crowd.

Franklin turns back around and continues to walk when he sees his father coming out of the main office. Franklin is completely caught off guard.

"Dad?"

Dr. Fulani's eyes comb the hallway. Being a little preoccupied, he only glances down at his son and then quickly raises his eyes back up to scan.

"Hey, Franklin."

He's dressed in his usual work attire but has a different look on his face that is unrecognizable. His eyes have the look of a madman who's desperately trying to hold on to whatever sanity he has left.

Being pulled into his father's web of paranoia, Franklin's eyes take a quick sweep around him. "What are you doing here? Is everything okay?"

"I'm here having a meeting with the principal and superintendent. Donating a little money to the booster club."

"You look like there's something wrong." Franklin becomes curious as to why his father doesn't look at him but obsessively eyes every student who passes by.

Being somewhat lost in his own world, Dr. Fulani slowly mumbles, "Ara ara ko ni pinya."

"What?"

Continuously blinking his eyes and shaking his head, he snaps out of the state of mind that he's in and looks down at his son. "Nothing… nothing. What are you doing?"

"I finished eating lunch and am heading to my next class."

"Good… good. I'm going back to work for a while." Dr. Fulani turns and starts to walk away.

Never having seen his father in this state before, Franklin was completely puzzled while watching his father walk away. Dr. Fulani takes one last suspicious gander over his shoulders before pushing through the glass door leading outside.

26
FAUSTIN

Johns Hopkins Hospital

The workday is close to being finished, but Faustin decides to head out a little early, seeing there are no more patients who he has to tend to for the day. In his office, he organizes his desktop for the next workday and closes out his web browser on his computer before turning the lights off and shutting the door.

"See you Monday, Doctor Nwaike." A nurse walks past him with a stack of folders to file.

"Okay! I'll see you on Monday. Have a nice weekend."

He walks, blowing a big gust out of his mouth as if some weight has been lifted off of his shoulders. People from his team clean up their work areas to complete the day as he walks away. He tiredly but consistently throws his hand up and waves at each person who passes by.

In the parking lot, he casually strolls to his vehicle, twirling his keys around his finger through the key ring. He pops his car door open and hops in while another car pulls into the parking space beside him. It's Doctor Fulani's car, and he opens the door, displaying himself as he exits.

Faustin slowly pulls into the driveway of the house, eyeing the outside perimeter as well as the windows the entire time. The previous day's discovery in the basement has him a little paranoid. He comes to a smooth halt and cuts the engine off. He quietly watches the windows and outside, looking for any abnormal movement.

His head quickly jerks to the side, trying to figure out a faint noise behind his car. It's only a neighboring mother and her child walking past the house.

In the house, Jeanine sits upright on the living room sofa looking like she's a little on edge and also still shaken by the previous day's discovery. She hugs a couch pillow as she watches the news, trying to hear anything about the babysitter that they discovered in the basement in hopes of finding out a little more about her.

The door swings open, and Faustin walks in. He notices the darkness in the rear of the house from all of the lights being off and then notices his wife on the sofa.

He quietly closes the door. "Hey!"

"Hey!"

"Where's Odo?" He sits his bag in front of the coat rack and hangs his jacket on it.

"He's sleeping right now."

He takes one more look at the darkness in the rear of the house and then back at his wife before walking toward the sofa. "Is everything okay?"

She nods. "Uh-huh."

He gently flops on the sofa next to his wife, and they share a quick kiss before he tunes into the news with her.

Of the different stories and updates that the news shows, only one of them stands out to the couple. It's an update on the teen girl whose limbs had been removed and was discovered in a nearby alley. Her name was Jessica Francisco, and the photo that's shown is Jessica, the babysitter.

"Oh my God…Oh my God…Oh my God!" Jeanine shoves the couch pillow into the sofa cushion beside her and erects her body toward the television.

"What? What is it?" Faustin joins her, moving the same way, but is confused about why she's excited.

Jeanine doesn't answer Faustin right away and listens to a little more of the update.

So far, the police don't have any leads based on any kind of forensic evidence. There is no trace of DNA or fingerprints. The only blood found at the scene was of the victim, and the only witness was not there during the killing. He is a homeless man who only discovered the body.

"That's the babysitter."

Faustin gently rubs his wife's back. "No…no. The babysitter died in the basement. Remember?"

"No, I'm talking about the young babysitter who never came that day. Jessica."

Not knowing how to take all of the news in, Jeanine sits there shaking her head in disbelief at the television. Faustin continuously rubs her back to give her some comfort.

Later that night, Faustin and Jeanine lie in bed. The moonlight dives through the cracked window as the soft wind causes the curtain to wave. Jeanine is completely sound asleep and lying halfway on her husband's chest. He is in somewhat of a twilight stage of sleep that's between deep sleep and being awake. His mind is away from the world, but his eyes are cracked slightly open.

The remembrance of Hazel's death streams through his thoughts as he remembers himself looking around the house on that day. The memory of the back door being cracked open shoots through his mind followed by the sight of Hazel's dangling feet three feet off of the floor. His memory scans the details of the floor. There was nothing below her feet for a woman, who could barely walk, to stand on to hang herself.

With his eyes still cracked open, his mind slowly comes back to the world, and he faintly notices the room around him. Its shadowy dark blue has a still silence that is somewhat eerie. The curtains continue to wave from the night breeze, causing movement on the wall. Each wave of the curtain darkens the spot on the wall over and over. At the foot of the bed, there's a view of the wide-opened bedroom doorway that allows the short hallway to be seen.

Another shadowy wave from the curtain and a silhouette of a person standing in front of little Odo's door, facing inside. It's unclear who it is, but it is not Odo.

Faustin's eyes open fully, and he jumps up out of bed, tossing Jeanine to the other side. He rushes out of the room to the spot where the silhouette of the person was standing. A quick click of the light and a look into his son's room reveals nothing out of the ordinary. His son sleeps soundly with no disturbance. Panting from the excitement, he scurries to the top of the stairs and, looks down into the darkness and sees nothing.

"What is it? What's wrong?" Jeanine sits at the foot edge of the bed, yelling through the doorway.

"It's nothing. Everything is fine."

He takes one more glance in his son's room to make sure he's safely sleeping and clicks off the light before walking back toward his bedroom. Walking through the bedroom doorway, he turns and pushes the door open as wide as it can possibly open and then crawls into bed. He adjusts his body directly in the line of the doorway in order to be able to see clearly down the hallway. Finally placing his head on his pillow, he constantly pops it up every several seconds, taking a peek down the hallway until he finally sets his head on the pillow for the final time that night.

The bright morning comes, and Jeanine slowly raises her head from her pillow to muffled thudding in the hallway. On his knees, the bottom half of Faustin's body protrudes out of the hallway closet while he rummages for something.

"What are you doing?"

Hearing his wife's voice causes his motion to freeze for a second, and then continue rummaging.

"I'm looking for something." He stands up and starts searching on the overhead shelf and sees the black backpack that has the amulet in it.

He hears Jeanine slide out of bed and starts to hurry, reaching inside and feeling around for something. He pulls out the rusted-looking necklace and amulet charm that John gave him and shoves it in his pants pocket a split-second before Jeanine rounds the edge of the closet door.

"Good morning." He tries to keep her oblivious to the charm of being in the house.

"Good morning." She gives him a kiss and proceeds to the bathroom to start her shower water.

Odo comes out of his room and joins his father. Faustin picks him up for a kiss before carrying him downstairs.

Toys are scattered everywhere on the living room floor as he carries his son to the sofa.

"One of these days, I'm going to slip and fall because of these things on the floor." He gently kicks the toys to the side, creating a path to the sofa.

"I'm going to turn on some cartoons, start some breakfast, and then pick up all of these toys…with your help." He places his son on the sofa.

Leaning down to click on the television, he turns around and scans the living room mess on the floor. He notices something under the sofa that looks like a black container and reaches for it. It's the black container that Charlena pushed under the sofa to hide, but he doesn't know who left it.

He curiously examines the outside of it before slowly and very cautiously opening it. Bringing it up to his nose, he softly sniffs and then jerks away from the rancid and rotting smell. Little Odo knows where it came from but can't say anything.

He walks into the kitchen and tosses the black container into the trash can.

27
FRANKLIN

Fulani Residence

Franklin buoyantly bounces down the stairs of his father's half-mansion. He gets to the bottom of the stairs and sees his father in his office, sitting at his desk with his back turned to the door. Umar looks as though he's seen better days with his hair wild and uncombed. He slouches and seems to be slowly flipping through a large book of photos. It's out of Umar's character to be this way.

"Hey, Pop!"

Continuing to flip through the book that's in front of him, Dr. Fulani takes another three to four seconds before letting out a miserable-sounding and drawn-out response. "What?"

Franklin notices the change in his father but brushes it off like it's nothing and asks a question that his father always says no to.

"I was wondering if I could borrow the car real quick?"

While his father contemplates, Franklin grimaces, holding on to a little hope that he will let him use the car.

His father lets out another drawn-out response. "Sure."

Franklin quickly snatches the keys off of the tall oak side table that's posted by the door and grabs the doorknob.

"HEY!" Umar doesn't turn around but only turns his head to the side. Franklin jumps back.

"Be safe."

Franklin nods. "I will."

In his father's luxury Audi, the blare of gangster rap vibrates the windows and causes anything loose to rattle around. Franklin bounces his head up and down like the typical teen boy listening to music.

He pulls into the mall parking lot and parks the car while continuing to blare the music, trying to look impressive to a group of high school girls walking by. He shuts the car off and exits.

It's not the typical Saturday at the mall. It's dead, and some of the stores haven't even opened yet. Franklin casually strolls through it, seeming to be looking for a particular store and comes to a bench to sit on. He keeps eyeing the The Streets' Finest clothing store that still has its security gate down but has employees moving around inside, preparing to open.

"Ain't nothing going on up in here today. Not a damn thing," he mumbles to himself.

He visually scans around until the security gates on the clothing store start to rise. Quickly jumping off of the bench, he tries to keep calm and cool while rushing to get there before anyone else.

A high school-aged roaming employee greets him with a head nod as he enters. Franklin heads straight for the section that has t-shirts.

"Welcome! Let me know if you need anything or if you're looking for anything in particular." Another employee walks past him.

Franklin sighs and shakes his head slightly, seemingly annoyed at the greeting already.

He pulls a t-shirt off of the rack and holds it up to himself. The shirt is a solid black shirt with a breast pocket. It's nothing fancy, but it seems to have caught Franklin's eye. "Yeah, this is nice."

He hears what sounds like another employee offering assistance behind him but in an overdone feminine voice. "Yes, you would look really sexy in that shirt."

Extremely bothered, he turns around to the strange voice and finds three black teenage boys laughing and joking around. Recognizing the boys, he quickly lightens his mood and starts snickering with them with some fist bumps.

"What ya'll doing?"

"Chillin' today…like everybody else." One of the boys seems a little rambunctious and over the top with excitement.

Filled with the glee of seeing some old friends again, Franklin displays the biggest smile on his face that hasn't been there in a long time.

"Nigga, we was wondering where you been. Why you leave Dunbar?"

Franklin rolls his eyes. "Man, my dad pulled me up outta there. Put me in Roosevelt."

"Roosevelt?"

"Yep! It's aight there, though. It ain't as snobby as everybody thinks," Franklin assures.

His friends nod with understanding.

Later that hour, they sit on a bench outside of the stores, cackling and catching up with each other. There's a thicker crowd than earlier at the mall as more people are shopping.

"When they brought Garrad out of the office in those cuffs, he was crying like a bitch." One of the boys leans in and speaks with heavy emphasis.

Franklin has tears in his eyes from laughing so much. "So Garrad got caught trying to fuck Ashley?"

"Yep!"

Franklin remembers the time that Principal Garrad confronted him about the nude picture of an underage student. "It was that picture. I knew he kept it and kept looking at it. Made him wanna hit it."

"And that little ho was down too."

"I'm not surprised."

Their laughter slowly calms from the story before Franklin remembers more students from his old high school. "What's going on with Jemar and them boys he runs with?"

One of the boys gives a slight twist of the lips and a shake of the head. "Nothin'. Still up to the same bullshit. Niggas always trying to act hard."

Something behind Franklin catches the eyes of his old friends. They all cease in laughter, and their eyes raise with curiosity.

"What's up, brah?" One of the friends feels a little paranoid.

Franklin turns around and notices Lukozi standing over him. He's dressed in nice slacks and a button-down shirt that's tightly tucked in, not looking much like a teenage boy on a Saturday. He looks a little intimidated to approach them but keeps a strained smile on his face and a look of desperation to join in.

Having his mind caught up in old memories with some old friends, Franklin hesitates to recognize the boy behind him. "Oh! What's up, man?"

"Franklin, do you know this nigga?"

Franklin rises out of his seat to introduce Lukozi to the rest of his friends. "Yeah! This is Lukozi here. He goes to Roosevelt with me."

Franklin's friends twist their faces and look Lukozi up and down, silently scoffing as if he's not good enough to join them.

"He's cool peoples, though," Franklin reassures their cool status while being seen with him.

They give in and trust Franklin's comforting words. "Aight, if you say so."

Knowing Lukozi's awkwardness, Franklin offers the seat he was sitting in to get more adjusted to the conversation. Lukozi sits with the stiffness and uprightness of someone trying very hard not to move the wrong way or look bad in front of new people.

"Hello! What's up?" He speaks in a manner of one who's trying to sound similar to his peers but struggles to put the words together.

The boys stare at him, trying to figure him out. One of them eyes his clothes. "You do know it's a Saturday, right?"

Confused about what the boy is talking about, Lukozi looks down at his clothes and back up at the boy.

Quickly intervening, Franklin nervously covers for Lukozi's lack of knowledge on cool and relaxing clothes. "Yeah, my man is always dressed for business."

Lukozi notices the relaxed slouch posture of the boys compared to his stiffness and starts fidgeting around, trying to adjust himself to a similar look. He struggles to slump his back down to avoid looking so uptight. Instead, he looks as though he's trying to do crunches. His elbow gets placed on his knee and then taken off of his knee. He doesn't really know what he wants to do. Meanwhile, the boys sit in silence and watch his awkward attempt to transition the entire time.

One of the boys has had enough of the show and decides to change subjects. "I'm hungry as hell. Y'all hungry?"

Each one blurts out in response, except for Franklin. Remembering Lukozi's abnormal eating habits from the school lunchroom, Franklin quickly tells the guys he's not hungry, trying to prevent them from seeing Lukozi eating.

"You ain't gotta eat nothing, nigga. We can all eat. You can watch." The boys cackle.

He rolls his eyes and sighs, giving in and going along with the eating plans as they get up and start walking.

"I don't even think nothin's open right now." Franklin tries to convince the boys to do something else one more time.

They spot a Mexican food shop opening its doors. Filled with a little excitement, one of the boys gives a loud clap of the hands before pointing at the food shop.

"Bam! There it go."

After they get their food and have a seat at the table, they immediately start shoveling food into their mouths. Trying to stay cautious of Lukozi's ability to cause people's stomachs to churn due to his eating, Franklin nibbles on his food and nervously keeps his eyes on his friend from Roosevelt. He doesn't want his friends from Dunbar to be repulsed and scared away. Lukozi eats somewhat normally as he continues to try to mirror the rest of the boys in every way, trying to fit in.

"So what's up, man? What's going on over there at Roosevelt?" one of the boys from Dunbar mumbles with food clogging his mouth.

Franklin picks at his food. "Absolutely nothin'. It's kinda boring. We did have a guy killed, though."

Another one of the boys elevates his tone with a little excitement and pauses his eating. "Yo, somebody knifed him at school or something?"

"Nah! Outside of school somewhere."

The boy's excitement quickly calms, and he continues eating. The entire table devours the rest of their meals in a carnivorous way with no talking until they're finished.

Sitting back, belching and filled with all kinds of gas, the boys start to relax and chitchat a little.

"So why'd ya pops take you out of Dunbar?"

"He tried to keep me in. Garrard's the one who booted me out." Franklin crumples up his trash.

Lukozi sits and listens to the conversation without saying a word. He feels like he's one of the guys.

One of the boys chuckles, "Well, you see where Garrard is now."

The boys chuckle at the thought of their old principal being in a worse place. One of the boys gets up and throws his trash into the nearby trash can. "I'm surprised he wasn't scared of yo pops and let you stay in."

"Garrad wanted me out no matter what."

"Yeah, but yo pops be coming off as some old big African…jabali nigga."

The rest of the guys bust out a loud cackle while Lukozi forces his laugh, not actually understanding the joke.

Lukozi's forced smile slowly starts to fade into a serious look of concern. He rapidly jumps out of his seat, causing the rest of the jumps to flinch and stop the conversation.

"You aight?" Franklin looks up at him.

Lukozi doesn't say a word and simply walks out, leaving the boys stunned at his awkwardness.

"What's up with ya, man? Yo, he's weird as hell."

Franklin continues to eye the exit where Lukozi darted out. "Nah! He aight."

The boys from Dunbar have a look on their faces as if Franklin is full of it but never says a word, challenging Franklin's friendship with Lukozi.

All is quiet as a mouse in the Fulani house; one could hear a pin drop. Everything is dead still, until a shadow appears in front of the front door of someone on the porch. The door eases open with absolutely no sound, and Franklin creeps in with a very soft heel-to-toe walk, trying to stay as quiet as possible. He slowly shuts the door and quietly places the key back on the table without making any jingle at all. He takes one step toward the stairs.

"Where have you been?" His father's voice rumbles through the house and echoes off of the walls.

Not knowing where his father is, Franklin freezes with his eyes continuously shifting around. "I was at the mall."

There's a long pause of silence, waiting for a response from Dr. Fulani before Franklin grows enough courage to take another step.

"Why were you gone for so long?"

Franklin apprehensively stutters, trying to think of anything he can say as an excuse. His father casually steps from around the corner, having the same unkempt hair as he did when Franklin left the house. The serious scowl on his face forces its way through the scruffiness of his unshaven face.

"Who were you with?" Dr. Fulani's elevated tone in his voice drops to a very calm and almost silent level.

Franklin's eyes are widened with fear, not ever seen his father in this state of mind before. Not knowing the repercussions of a possible wrong answer, he hesitates to speak. Dr. Fulani takes a couple of steps toward Franklin.

"I was with some friends," Franklin quickly blurts.

With bloodshot eyes, Dr. Fulani silently glares at Franklin for several seconds, trying to read him. The glare is of a thousand-yard stare that shoots straight through Franklin's eyes.

"Okay!" He softly nods and walks back into the other room that he came from.

Franklin drops his shoulders and breathes a sigh of relief before heading upstairs.

28
FAUSTIN/JEANINE

Nwaike Residence

The sun shines brightly through the living room window with the curtains wide open. It's almost blinding light that limits the view of the surrounding scenery if you're facing the window.

Faustin finishes picking up the remaining toys while his son sits on the sofa watching him instead of the cartoons on the television.

"Thanks for your help picking up your toys." He points one of the little toys at Odo as the little one giggles.

"Breakfast is almost ready," Jeanine yells from the kitchen.

He notices one last toy directly below the window that the bright light beams through and bends down to pick it up. He rises back up and almost jumps out of his skin at the sight of Charlena standing on the other side of the window with an inanimate look on her face. He looks back toward the living room floor and observes only his shadow that can be seen and no one else's. The doorbell rings, and he quickly looks back toward the window to find Charlena gone.

The look on his face is of complete concern as he stands in the same spot without moving an inch. There is something within him that says something is strange about this. He is frozen, and his legs feel bolted to the floor as the doorbell rings again.

Jeanine walks in from the kitchen, wiping her hands off with a dish towel and proceeds to the front door. "What are you doing? Why don't you get the door?"

She opens the door and finds Charlena standing with a pleasant smile. Jeanine can't bring a smile to her face due to the uneasy feeling in her stomach that Charlena gives her. Jeanine's blank, and even a little worried-looking, face stares at Charlena for a couple of seconds without saying anything.

"I'm sorry to bother you, but…" Charlena speaks very pleasantly, overdoing it.

Faustin slowly steps from behind the door.

"Can…Can we help you?" Having an uneasy feeling as well, Faustin seems a little timid to speak.

"Yes, I think I left something here the last time I was here."

"We don't have it here." Faustin doesn't know what she's talking about but only tries to get her to leave.

"Sure, you do." Without being invited in, Charlena starts to step inside the house when she's abruptly halted in her tracks by something that she senses in the air. Her flaring nostrils guide her face around until they end aimed toward Faustin's pants pocket.

Within a split-second, her pleasant demeanor shifts to wretched. Her eyes quickly become beady as her breathing becomes labored and wheezy. She tries to push forward into the house, but her feet slide backward, almost struggling to lift off of the ground. She lets out a big screeching roar as she reaches out toward the shocked couple. The door slams shut, and Odo starts crying from the loud noise.

Faustin and Jeanine stand there breathing profusely from the fear of the moment before he scurries over to the window to close the curtain. As he's about to jerk it closed, he looks over and notices that she's not there anymore.

"Where'd she go?"

Jeanine rushes over to pick up the baby into her arms and starts hugging him to calm his fears. Faustin pulls the curtain closed.

Later that day, Jeanine is in the kitchen washing dishes. Every few seconds, she nervously keeps looking out of the kitchen window and into the backyard. Poking her head around the corner to the living room, she sees the back of her son's head as he's glued to the television set. She continues washing dishes and leaning around the corner to ensure her son's safety.

Faustin bounces down the stairs and takes a peek through the front door window before heading into the kitchen. He notices Jeanine's paranoia and doesn't wonder why because he already knows why.

"Is everything okay?" He cautiously glances over her shoulder and out of the kitchen window.

She nods and continues to wash dishes before he walks over to the backdoor and visually scans the yard. Her eyes drift off to the side and away from her task as her mind becomes invaded with a thought. She glances back and forth at him and the dishes. Then she drops her eyes to his pants pocket with a look of curiosity as he walks back toward the kitchen table and sits down.

"Stand back up, please." She slides the dish that she's holding back into the steamy water and dries her hands with the dish towel.

"What?"

She walks over to him, and he looks up at her as she gives him orders. "Stand up for a second. I want to see something."

He slowly stands up, and she quickly reaches into his pants pocket to feel around.

"She was looking at your pants," Jeanine's curiosity peaks.

She pulls out the necklace with the amulet charm and holds it up to her face. She bites her lip and shakes her head.

Faustin tries to calm Jeanine before she explodes into a rage. "Look, I know you said that you don't want this—"

She cuts him off. "It's okay. It's okay."

He gently grabs it from her hand and slides it back into his pocket. She goes back to washing the dishes and can be heard sniffling as if she's tearing up. He watches her closely as he sits back down.

"We have to keep Odo close to us." He tries to comfort her with reassuring words.

She never responds but keeps washing the dishes.

The dark night arrives, and the chirping crickets outside allow an easy and normal feeling to the exterior of the house. A couple of neighbors walk past the house and the rest of the neighborhood seem to be oblivious to the tension going on in one of their community's houses. Having no fences that separate the yards, the Nwaike house still seems to be completely isolated from the rest of the neighborhood.

Inside the dark house, a silent panic is brewing, with Faustin posted at the front window, propping the curtain open. He quietly and meticulously scans the yard and beyond. There's nothing out of the ordinary, so he closes the curtain and rids the downstairs of the only light that was in the lower level of the house. He proceeds toward the stairs, stopping by the front door to jiggle and yank on the knob. It's locked, so he starts ascending the stairs.

Upstairs in the lamp-lit bedroom, Jeanine lies motionless with her eyes wide open and staring at her son while he soundly sleeps in the middle of the bed next to her. She hears footsteps coming up the stairs and suspiciously lifts her head to look. Faustin reaches the top, and finally realizing that the noise is nothing to be afraid of, she drops her head back down on the pillow.

Faustin enters the bedroom, leaving the door wide open, and carefully places the charm at the foot of the bed before tiresomely sitting on his side of the bed. He rolls his neck around in a circle, stretching out the day's tension and turns to glance at his wife. She has quickly fallen asleep.

With a click of the lamp light, he pulls the covers back and slides the rest of himself into the bed. His body starts to roll over to face his family and is abruptly interrupted halfway when he notices the dark silhouette standing at the stairhead staring at them. He freezes with a quick hold of his breath before jerking back around to click on the light.

"What? What's there?" Jeanine is startled by her husband's sudden movements.

Faustin sees nothing at the stairhead while the light is on. "Nothing!"

He slowly gets out of bed and tiptoes through the bedroom door, grabbing the amulet and looking around every corner. His hands can't stop trembling, and the palpitations of his heart race as he starts to reach the top of the staircase. He steadily leans around the corner and gazes into the downstairs darkness but doesn't see anything.

Very concerned, Jeanine sees her son sleeping peacefully and completely oblivious to the surrounding worries. The opened bedroom door starts to ease shut without making a sound. It goes unnoticed because her attention is focused on Odo, and Faustin still leans his head toward downstairs, squinting to see any movement in the dark.

"My precious son," she whispers to herself and leans down to give him a kiss.

The lamp light starts to flicker, and Jeanine's eyes quickly shoot up toward it. In the blurry background, an incoherent figure starts to emerge from behind the closing door. Noticing from out of the corner of her eye, she slowly and cautiously rotates her head in that direction.

The lamp light stops flickering and cuts off completely. The only light in the room is a strip of moonlight shooting through the window and hitting the very spot where the incoherent figure stands. The rest of the room is total blackness.

Her eyes grow twice the size as a bug-eyed Charlena stands there. Charlena's eyes bulge out of her head, and her starving smile of dripped saliva displays jagged and corroded teeth. She stares at a sleeping Odo as if there is nothing human behind her eyes.

Jeanine wants to scream, but the sight of what's in front of her shocks her to silence.

Completely oblivious to the action in the bedroom behind him, Faustin continues to squint and sees nothing downstairs. The door closes completely, and the click grabs his attention. He quickly takes one step, trying to get back to the door, and something grabs his wrist. Whatever or whoever's holding on can't be seen, and Faustin only sees his arm, with indentations from a tight grip, trying to break free from the air. Not being able to see what's holding onto his wrist only causes his panic to intensify. He jerks and leans his body away, desperately trying to break free.

In the bedroom, Charlena stares at the sleeping baby, completely obsessed. Totally frozen from fear, Jeanine cautiously watches every move that she takes.

Her mind is hit with a memory as she notices something familiar about Charlena. Her thoughts flash back to the night that she gave birth to Odo at Reddington Hospital in Lagos. She focuses on the moment of the strange nurse approaching John with great interest and then walking away. The time is a little hazy to her, but she remembers that moment very clearly.

Charlena starts to take tiny steps toward the bed, and Jeanine bursts out in a loud scream. She clutches a waking Odo very tightly in her arms as he cries from fear of the abrupt, loud noise. The child's cries only entice Charlena more as her body slowly disappears out of the strip of light and into the blackness of the room.

In the hallway, Faustin panically tries to break free from what's holding his arm. He quickly pulls his other hand around to get more force to pull with and is released before he can grab his arm. Astonished at how fast he was released, he holds his helping hand up to his face and observes the mysterious amulet taking effect.

Ice-cold breaths of something within inches of him start to blow on his skin as a low, hollow-sounding howl of wind gust gently climbs the black staircase. He only feels the eeriness and hears the uneasiness, seeing nothing.

Quickly holding the amulet in front of him, he rapidly backs up toward the bedroom door and tries to turn the knob to open it. It's stuck, so he starts to kick it with the bottom of his shoe.

The loud banging on the door causes the baby's cries to intensify into a high wail as the sight of Charlena is completely swallowed by the shadows. Jeanine barely sees small parts of her slowly floating closer but can't clearly see how close she is. The air gets colder with each step that she takes.

There's a pause of complete silence in the room, with the exception of the banging on the door. Charlena no longer moves closer, but her whereabouts in the room are unknown. Jeanine's eyes scan the pitch black, quietly searching for any sign of Charlena.

"Hello, little one," a voice whispers from somewhere in the room.

Little Odo's eyes look up from being tucked in his mother's arms, and focus on one spot in the room. His mother glances down at him and sees the direction in which he's looking. She focuses in the same direction but struggles to see anything except total black.

Charlena can be heard playfully teasing the young one as he giggles. He starts to wipe the tears from his eyes and clears his heart of the fear that was there before.

Jeanine still scans the blackness, squinting to see anything that her son sees. She sees nothing.

Odo's gentle laughs start to grow dark as whimpering starts to take over. His whimpering elevates to a fearful cry, and Jeanine clutches him tighter as she feels a cold tensing of her skin as if something is reaching out to touch her.

The door bursts open, and Faustin clicks on the light. Jeanine quickly looks around, but nobody else is in sight. Panting from the rush, Faustin scurries over to check the window. It's closed and locked. He checks the closet, but there is nothing but clothes inside. Then he drops down and lifts the dangling blanket up to check under the bed and sees nothing. It's almost as if Charlena has vanished into thin air as soon as the light clicked on.

Faustin walks around the bed and sits on the edge to hold his weeping family tightly.

"What's going on?" Jeanine weeps.

"I think it's actually happening. I think the Abiku is trying to get Odo," Faustin says.

29
UMAR

Johns Hopkins Hospital

Monday morning, doors open at the hospital, and everyone's preparing for the day. The nurses scramble to get incoming patients' files in order. The clerk cleans and organizes the front counter while a hard buff is being polished on the waiting area marble floor.

Fancy black office clogs clack across the marble floor as a man walks over it. His suit is stained and wrinkled. The collared shirt under his blazer is partially tucked, with the tie only slung around his neck. His hair is wild and uncombed.

As he walks by clerks, nurses, and technicians, his unkempt look draws strange looks.

"Are you okay, Doctor?" A passing nurse moves to the side and out of his way.

The doctor opens his office door, shoving it until it hits the back wall and sits down in his chair. It's Dr. Fulani, and he stares at his reflection through a black computer screen on his desk.

A nurse silently and cautiously creeps behind the wall, not yet revealing herself in the office doorway.

"Can you get me some coffee, please, Cindy?" Knowing that she's there without seeing her, he calmly asks for his morning joe.

She nervously jumps in the doorway to reveal herself. "Yes, sir. It's coming right up."

He continues to stare at himself through the black computer screen. He sees a piece of the white wall within inches behind him start to slowly shift and twist as though the steel and drywall are softening up into play-dough. An imprint of something starts to push through. The further through that it pushes, the more it expands downward until the imprint is about sixty inches tall. It's noticeably a young boy, as the doctor's eyes flicker from the excitement.

Panicking, he jerked around to face the wall behind him to see that it was all in his imagination. Breathing heavily from the fear of the moment, he visually inspects the wall to see that it's still solid with no imprint.

"You have everyone concerned." A voice standing at the door causes the doctor to rotate back around in his chair. It's the medical director at Johns Hopkins.

Dr. Fulani stares at him with glazed eyes and without saying a single word. The medical director steps in and closes the door behind him. Standing in front of Dr. Fulani's desk, he sternly gazes into his eyes.

Umar knows the reason for the meeting but doesn't say anything. He waits, through the long and uncomfortable silence, for the medical director to open his mouth.

"I think you know why I'm here."

Dr. Fulani still stares silently.

"You're not completely focused on your job anymore. Your bodily functions are not steady when performing your tasks. You completely ignore your patients when they need your help…"

Dr. Funlani sits motionless and expressionless.

"And now you're starting to show up to work like this. Very unprofessional."

Dr. Fulani looks down at his dress attire and shrugs. "I don't see anything wrong with my clothes."

"I think you should take some time off."

"Am I being fired?"

"I think you should take some time away from work to gather yourself."

Dr. Fulani drops his head and starts to drum his fingers on the edge of the desk as he contemplates his next move.

"I will have all of your patients assigned to other physicians in the meantime."

No longer having the strong and stern look that he once possessed, he stands up with his head hanging low and his eyes on the floor. He starts to walk out of the office, looking like a man defeated by his own inner demons.

Behind him, the medical director pulls his nameplate off of his office door. One by one, the medical staff stops in their tracks and watches him as he shamefully walks out.

30
FRANKLIN

Roosevelt High School

Before the classes start for the day, students casually stroll into the building. Nobody is in a hurry to get to their first class, but the faces on several of the students and the slumped-over body language as they walk show that it is a painful necessity.

"What's up?" Franklin stands out of a passing herd that's on their way inside.

"Hey!"

He slows down enough to speak but keeps moving with the crowd. She continues to relax before the stress of school.

Inside the building, the flow of students is continuous with no change of pace. Franklin heads straight to his locker to lighten the load in his backpack. He's looking around him and further down the hallway as if he's searching for someone.

The last few students are arriving for a class as another bell rings. The teacher heads to the door to close it, and Franklin darts from around the corner and pokes his head in.

"Excuse me!"

The teacher puts her hands up, trying to keep Franklin out of the class that he doesn't belong in. "Can I help you?"

He leans in and sees the students all pulling out their books and preparing for class, but Lukozi's seat remains empty.

"Sorry!" He walks away from the door, leaving the teacher bewildered at his sudden appearance and departure.

Later in the day, the lunchroom is as packed as usual. The room no longer has a division based on skin color, and everyone sits comfortably in sections that they usually never sit in. Students who at first looked down on other students are now greeting them with a smile.

Franklin sits among a mixed group but at the same time in a space of his own. He has no conversation with anyone and constantly lifts his head up and scans around him, searching for his African friend.

There's a calendar on the wall behind the lunchroom cashier. Days that have gone by have been checked off as completed. One by one, checks appear on the present day and three days after as the school week progresses.

At his locker, while in between periods, he swaps out books for another class and glances over to the side. He notices the back of Lukozi's head, looking down at something. A cell phone in his hand pokes out from around his body as he fiddles with it. Franklin snickers and shuts his locker door.

He approaches his African friend from behind. "Man, when did you get a cell—"

He stops short as the boy turns around and shows that he's not Lukozi.

"My bad!" Franklin walks away, shaking his head from embarrassment.

On his way to enter his next class, he quickly backtracks when he notices Raven coming down the hallway with earbuds in her ear and approaches her.

"Have you seen Luke anywhere?"

"Who?" She pulls one of the earbuds out.

"Lukozi!"

Her eyes squint, trying to figure out who Franklin's talking about. "I don't even know who that is."

"The African kid I always hang with?"

She recollects, "I haven't seen him all week."

Franklin sighs and rolls his eyes. "Yeah, me neither."

He throws up his hand, waving goodbye, and she smiles as she shoves the earbuds back in and keeps walking.

Later in class, the teacher goes over a few important topics in class while Franklin slouches into his desk that's next to the window. He jots in his notebook but doesn't seem to really be interested in the class.

His mind starts to slip into another world, and his eyes follow as they drift over toward the window. The road has the occasional vehicle passing by, but what catches his attention is the tree line on the other side of the road. A young elementary school-aged black boy at the edge of the tree line and with his back turned to the school. The boy wears a shiny green and white shirt and is on his knees as if he is praying.

He's by himself, and, one by one, the vehicles on the road pass by as if they don't even see him. The final vehicle passes, and in a split-second, the boy disappears. The bush in the tree line doesn't move as if he jumped in, and Franklin scans from left to right, looking to see if he got up and ran away. He sees nothing. It's as if the boy was never there.

He turns back toward the class, and through the opened doorway, his eyes are grabbed by the same shiny green and white shirt leaving the doorway. Franklin never sees the face and feels like while he is watching, he is also being watched. He has an uneasy feeling about it, but he keeps it subtle, not to bring attention. He aims his attention back toward the teacher.

31
FAUSTIN/JEANINE

Nwaike Residence

The night has fallen, and Faustin's car sputters into the driveway to a squeaking stop. The car shuts off, and there is nothing but complete silence in the air while no one exits the vehicle.

Inside the car, the focus is on the dark house as they stare at it through the front windshield without saying a single word.

"I'm sorry, but I couldn't stay in this house by myself." Jeanine breaks the long silence.

"It's okay. But we have to find somewhere else for you to go because you can't continue to spend the entire day in my office at work. It's very difficult for the boy." Faustin points to the back seat where Odo quietly sleeps.

They sit and stare at the house for a moment, hesitating to move from the car.

"It's okay. We can't sit out here forever." He cracks the car door open.

She turns around to a sleeping Odo and nudges him as he moans and groans. "Odo, we're home."

She exits the car and opens the back seat for her son while Faustin opens the driver's side back seat and grabs his work bag.

They casually walk toward the house as a family as Faustin reaches into his pocket for the house key. He accidentally pulls out the amulet charm with no necklace and slides it back in to pull the house key out of his other pocket.

Ascending the front porch steps, Faustin cautiously eyes the windows to see if he notices anything out of the ordinary. He inserts the key and turns the heavy bolt out of the frame and into the door. The doorknob only jiggles, and the spindle feels jammed by something in the borehole. Scooting tighter to the door, to get more power in his hands, he starts to use both hands to turn the knob before forcefully running his shoulder into the door.

"What the hell…" He steps back to assess the door.

Jeanine reaches in to check the doorknob and can't move it either. Faustin turns and starts walking back down the porch steps before cutting through the yard.

"Where are you going?" Jeanine pulls her hand away from the doorknob.

"I'm gonna try the back door." Faustin rounds the corner of the house and starts making his way down the side.

Odo looks up at his mother with big, sleepy eyes that he rubs.

"Don't worry. We'll get you inside. I know you're sleepy." She looks down at her son and snickers.

Rounding the back corner of the house, Faustin fights his way through the thick bush that protrudes over the walkway. He continuously stumbles over crunching twigs and other debris that cover the pavement.

From the front porch, Jeanine takes a gander around the dark neighborhood to see very few lights on, shining out of the neighboring homes. The normally comforting, complete silence causes a little bit of eeriness within her. She turns and tries the doorknob again, and the door cracks open.

Surprised at the sudden change in security, Jeanine hesitates to move before turning toward the side of the house to yell for her husband. "Faustin!" There's no response.

She slowly moves closer to the door and peeks through the crack. Nothing out of the ordinary is there, so she nudges the squeaking door open and stares into total blackness.

Behind the house, Faustin finally gets to the back door and tries to slide it open, but it's understandably locked. He scans the entire backside of the house and notices the kitchen window. After a few forceful tugs of the kitchen window, it stays stuck. He cuts his suspicious eyes back to the door and starts moving toward it.

Jeanine still stands at the door, hesitating to move across the threshold. She slowly leans in to get a closer view before stepping in and pulling Odo with her. She clicks the light switch, but nothing happens.

"Stay here." She gently pushes her son against the wall beside the door, keeping him in the moonlight while she scurries into the darkness to find the lamp.

Her hands guide her as she feels around in front of her to reach the lampshade and turn the switch. The click causes no difference in the lighting of the room.

What sounds like the back door sliding shut catches her attention, and her worries wash away as she takes a big sigh of relief.

The sound of Faustin's work shoes clacking on the hardwood floor echoes as he walks through from the back of the house. His slacks and work shirt dip into the strips of moonlight as he walks passed, but the light never reaches his face.

"You really didn't have to go around the back. All it took was a little extra effort, and the door popped open," she reassures him.

She continues to struggle to make her way around as she continues to take baby steps. "Come here, Odo. Be careful."

Faustin heads toward the door while Odo rushes over to his mother in a panic.

"It's okay, baby. Daddy will have the light on in a second." She tries to give Odo a little comfort.

"No!" Little Odo blurts out in a tiny voice.

Jeanine's sudden memory of parts of the house allows her to move around in the dark more easily than other parts. Odo follows uneasily. She hears Faustin following her and Odo.

"Faustin, try the breaker switch in the basement." She urges him to find a way to get the lights working again.

Faustin keeps quiet and keeps following the two of them. Jeanine finds that to be strange, and her concerns start to rise a little while doubt creeps into her mind that this is not Faustin. Her pull on little Odo's arm gradually becomes harder as her speed elevates, navigating through the dark. Panic starts to set in, but she keeps calm, desperately holding on to the hope of this being her husband, not knowing where he's going.

In the back of the house, Faustin continues to pull on the back door. He cups his hands to the side of his face while he presses against the glass to try to see in. He sees nothing but complete blackness and then faintly sees a silhouette standing directly on the other side of the door.

"What the hell? Jeanine? Is that you?" Faustin squints.

The silhouette starts to emerge more clearly from the other side of the window. It looks to be of a grown man with a familiar-looking face. Faustin leans in for a closer study of his face and sees very similar features of his son's face. The eyes stare into Faustin's eyes with unimaginable pain in them before slowly turning blood red. Tears of blood form and start to roll down the face of the man.

Faustin backs off of the window in awe and looks up to see the bedroom window.

Jeanine stops in her tracks as she loses sight of the silhouette that seemingly faded more into the dark. She stands there in complete stillness, holding onto her son's hand. Her eyes squint and scan the black to see nothing moving, and her breath is held in an attempt to hear anything that she can. The eeriness of someone close causes her body to feel a little chill.

The feeling of a little muscle strain sets in as she feels her arm getting tighter when her son tries to walk away.

"Hold on right here," she whispers to him as he continues to try to walk away.

Little Odo whimpers, "No!"

She whispers again, "Wait just a second, Odo."

"Stop it!"

The faintest and lowest whisper can be heard coming from Odo's direction. The whispers are so faint that it almost sounds like the sputter of the gentlest wind whistling.

Jeanine realizes that Odo is not trying to walk away—he's being pulled away. She jerks his arm toward her, and at the same time his other arm is being pulled in the other direction like a tug-of-war match. No other sound can be heard coming from the opponent as they compete for Odo. It's almost as if it's only the dark that's trying to take him.

Jeanine notices a single strip of moonlight shooting through the living room window and tries to target that location to pull her son. She wants to see what is trying to take him, but the strength of the opponent is too much.

Outside of the house, Faustin struggles to climb the guttering drain pipe that seems to be loose and breaking away from the outside wall. He reaches for the window ledge and pulls himself closer to the window to find out that it's unlocked. He slides it up.

Jeanine's struggle to pull her son loosens as they break free from the grasp of the dark and scurry toward the front door. The front door is locked, and in a panic, she pulls him up the stairs as the feeling of what's in the dark scampers after them.

At the top of the steps, she turns around and looks behind her to see Charlena standing in the strip of moonlight at the foot of the stairs, staring at them both. With frizzy and wild hair, she leers with hollowed eyes and cruddy teeth that look as though mud has been smeared all over them. Even from the distance of the flight of stairs, her chest can be seen expanding and contracting from intense breathing. Almost in slow motion, she calmly steps up on the first tread of the steps and out of the moonlight.

Jeanine scrambles to turn back around and run toward the bedroom, but she slips on the last tread of steps. She ends up on her knees with her torso barely around the corner from the last step, but her lower legs still extend over the step.

She looks over to Odo to nudge him further toward the room, but he stands there looking at the steps. Jeanine slowly turns back toward the steps and sees Charlena sitting on the top step, inches away from her legs. She looks pleasant but eerie. With a haunting smile on her face and normal-looking eyes again, she gives Jeanine a creepy, false sense of reassurance.

"It's going to be okay."

Jeanine quickly tries to get back to her feet and grabs Odo's arm at the same time. In a microsecond, Charlena's face flips back to the way that it was in the strip of moonlight, and she grabs Odo's other arm to pull him back toward the stairs.

Off balance from the attempt to get back to her feet, Jeanine falls back down as she clutches Odo's arm tightly. The animal strength of Charlena pulling Odo causes her to be dragged back to the center of the staircase.

Faustin struggles to squeeze through the partially opened bedroom window. His body hangs halfway out, and his legs dangle in the air. Twisting, turning, and jerking, he's not able to find anything to thrust himself further through the window, so he wiggles back and forth to use his body weight and gather slow momentum. The amulet charm falls out of his pocket and rolls across the bedroom floor and beside the door.

Being dragged halfway down the stairs, Jeanine pulls her knees to her chest to get back to her feet and maneuvers her way back to her feet. She finds extra strength out of love and the need to protect her son and slips out of Charlena's grasp.

She pulls Odo to the top of the stairs and around the corner to the opened bedroom door. She turns around and freezes to see nothing but completely dark calm.

Almost in slow motion, Charlena's face starts to protrude from around the corner of the stairhead and stops. Her hollowed eyes pierce through them as she remains completely motionless.

Standing in the bedroom doorway, Jeanine glances back to a thumping noise in the room to find Faustin climbing through it. The glance only took a split-second before Charlena's inches away and looking down toward Odo.

Jumping with shock and surprise, she jerks her son into the room and slams the door as Faustin drops from the window and to the floor. She scampers over to him and helps him to his feet, pulling Odo every inch of the way.

There's a long, gentle scratching sound slowly crawling down the door. Faustin and Jeanine stand there, gripping Odo tightly and trying to figure out their next move. He eyes back and forth through the window and the door, contemplating climbing down the side of the house.

"Quick! Through the window." He shoves his wife and son toward the window.

The amulet charm catches Faustin's eye, and he dashes to it for protection before the bedroom door shatters off of the hinges. Bits from the pine slab spray into Faustin, knocking him down to his face as a demonized Charlena calmly steps into the room.

Staring into Faustin's eyes with her own hollowed eyes, she takes one step across the bedroom threshold and screamingly darts for Odo without looking.

Terrified, Jeanine jumps in front of Odo to shield him and gets snatched by her throat and lifted up. Her feet dangle while she stares down into the two black holes that are staring back up at her.

Experiencing a slight similarity to paralysis in his body from shock, Faustin struggles to get back to his feet while scanning the floor for the amulet charm. It's nowhere to be found, and he wonders where it went as he stands back up.

Once gazing down into Charlena's face with tight-gripping hands wrapped around her neck, she finds herself slowly dropping to the floor, with the grip gradually loosening and eventually letting go.

A curiously frightened Jeanine backs against the wall, pushing Odo further back to keep him at a safe distance behind her.

Charlena looks down and notices the amulet charm poking out of the top of her foot. She starts to let out sickly sounds of gagging mixed with belching as the flesh of her foot melts into a small pile of maggots. She belches up a small amount of bloody vomit on her shirt before shrieking out an eardrum-bursting scream and throwing herself through the shattering glass of the bedroom window.

Faustin quickly rushes over to the window to see only the calm of the backyard. He doesn't see anything out of the ordinary except for the lack of a body lying there.

Odo goes around his mother to attempt to be close to his father, but Jeanine stops him in his tracks to keep him away from the pile of maggots. "Wait right here, Odo."

Faustin bends down, sweeps the maggots off of the amulet with his bare hands, and picks it up. He holds it up in between him and Jeanine to where the small amount of moonlight coming through the window hits it. "Do you still think it's voodoo?"

32
FRANKLIN

Fulani Residence

Later in the night, Franklin lies sprawled out in his bed. The blue moon pokes through the wide-open curtains, and shadows of tree branches wave across his room. He's sound asleep but still squirms around from the dream that he's having.

He's walking into the empty school parking lot with a lone black Hellcat parked. The hood is raised up with someone under it. As he gets closer to the car, the hood is slammed shut, revealing Thomas wiping off his hands.

"What do you want, faggot?" Thomas notices him approaching.

There's no reply from Franklin, and Thomas starts to scoff while walking toward the driver's side door, "You're fucking weird."

Franklin follows within inches behind him and places his hand on the car door as Thomas tries to open it.

"You better get the fuck off of my car before I beat your ass, you African chimp," Thomas becomes annoyed.

He steps into Franklin's face and gives an aggressive shove. An inhuman snarl causes Thomas to fearfully jump back.

Franklin lunges forward and starts chasing Thomas as he runs for his life.

He zigzags, trying to shake his chaser and yelling for help, but Franklin stays tight on him as he runs into the treeline.

Running deeper into the woods, Thomas trips on a fallen tree branch and falls to the ground as Franklin closes in on him.

He rolls over onto his back, and Franklin quickly straddles him with a hand clutching his face, pinning his head to the ground. Franklin rips Thomas' shirt from his chest like a beast and slices his stomach open with his fingernails. Blood starts to run out before he shoves his hand all the way in, causing a massive spurt. He starts to rip out his entrails as Thomas' yells become faint to the point of complete silence.

Thomas' dead-open eyes peek through Franklin's spread fingers, and the hand that is pinning his head down rips the skin off of his face with one jerk.

He flashes to walking through the school hallway. Several students give him a strange stare as they walk by him.

He leans around the corner and sees himself as an out-of-body experience. He's heading into a classroom but then backtracks to talk to Raven. He says something to her, and she pulls out her earbuds to hear him clearly. He says something again before she shakes her head. Franklin walks into the classroom while Raven continues down the hallway.

With a strange interest, his eyes zoom in on Raven while she walks away, and then he looks up to the overhead convex security mirror to see himself as a wild-eyed Lukozi.

Franklin jumps up out of his nightmare, panting and sweating profusely.

33
UMAR

Fulani Residence

It's midday, and Dr. Fulani sits in his dark home office in nothing but his underwear and bathrobe. The entire room is blackened, with the exception of a strip of blinding sunlight shooting through the window below the partially opened shade that's elevated about four inches.

Through the four inches, the bright world can be seen as neighbors joyfully walk their dogs and children laugh and play. Other neighbors mow their lawns and cause the beautiful smell of freshly cut grass.

In the home office, the darkness dampens any bright spirit that draws near and the cold lingers without any intent of leaving. The smell in the air is more putrid and almost similar to something rotting or decomposing.

Dr. Fulani sits back and stares blankly straight ahead. The vintage photo album that he was shuffling through before is on the desk in front of him. The delicate and soft sound of children laughing and talking faintly echoes through his head and gradually grows louder as his mind drifts into an old memory.

The big gates at a school in Kano, Nigeria, swing open, and children flood the walkway to leave for the day. Some of the children scurry to the vehicles of their parents while others walk to their nearby homes.

An eight-year-old Umar walks with his friend, who seems to be a little eccentric, donning an Igbo bucket hat pulled down to the top of his sunglasses that cover half of his face. The friend seems a little rambunctious as he bounces in his steps. Other groups of schoolchildren walk in front and back of them.

"I don't know about you, but Mrs. Adeoye is starting to make me mad with the homework," Umar tells his friend.

"I don't know why you're complaining. You're going to do it anyway. You always do." His rambunctious friend picks up a stick and starts swatting at the leaves on the trees as they pass by them.

Umar doesn't say a single word but keeps walking at a casual pace.

"Me, I don't really care. If she gives homework that I don't like, I just don't do it," the friend brags without a care in the world.

"Yes, I can tell by your grades."

"I'll leave the smarts to you, Umar. Not for me." He starts to twirl the stick as if it's a sword.

Umar swats his hand at dangling leaves. "One day, I will go to America to work. I will make sure you get there too because…"

"Awa ara ko ni pinya." The two boys turn toward each other and say in unison.

They notice a thick-shrubbed pathway that piques their interest, and no other student is taking. Stopping in their tracks and pulling to the side, they let the kids walking behind them pass by.

"Let's take this shortcut."

Umar feels unfamiliar with the pathway. "I don't know that way."

His friend feels bold and arrogant as he attempts to reroute their path home. "It's a faster way. Don't worry. I won't let nothing happen to you."

They start to walk downhill to the thick boscage, and the surroundings become more narrow until they approach a tiny opening to a path. The path is very slim, with rich shoulder-high combretum micranthum bushes lining each side. Small tumbled stones scatter in the dirt as they tread through the unknown area.

"I can't see anything in here." Umar jumps up and down, trying to peek over the bushes.

Going deeper into the path, the rich bushes start to become sickly-looking, with leaves falling off of the dying branches. The deeper the boys walk, the less appealing the bushes look until they come to an abrupt dead-end.

"You said this was a shortcut!" Umar shoves his friend.

"I thought it was."

Umar starts shaking his head in disappointment when his eyes catch a nearby shaded nook with patchy grass. Iroko trees tower around the nook, blocking out the beam of the sun, except for a few strips of light.

Umar becomes a little curious and starts to walk toward the secluded area while his friend turns and notices the place.

"What is that over there?" The friend starts to follow Umar.

"You tell me, since you're so familiar with this shortcut." Being upset with his friend's lies, Umar talks rudely to him.

Entering the nook, Umar approaches a strip of sunlight and stands there, squinting up at the dark trees to vaguely see tinker toys dangling from the branches.

"I can't see anything with these things on." The friend stands back in the shadows, pulls off his sunglasses, and adjusts his bucket hat to be able to see up into the trees better.

Complete calm and silence overrun the place without even hearing anything or anyone beyond the outer walls of the trees. It's as if the nook is only present for the two boys and completely cut off from the rest of the world.

The friend approaches a strip of sunlight next to Umar that is shooting through the trees, and Lukozi's face is plain as day as he gazes up at the trees with Umar. His face is young and fresh with all of the innocence that a kid can bare, but with a little adolescent mischievousness.

A small and slow rattling noise is heard from a dark corner that catches their attention. Someone stands in the dark, sounding as if they're adjusting something against the inner walls of the trees. Slightly hunched over and covered with an old ratty blanket draped over their head, the person limps further and further to the side as they tamper with the wall of trees.

The boys stay silent and frozen out of fear of being noticed. They glance at each other, contemplating what to do next before Lukozi quietly yanks on Umar's shirt to sway him into leaving.

"You're not going anywhere." The voice of the person sounds raspy and sickly.

The boys turn their heads to a light swishing sound of a bush moving behind them and turn their heads to see that the opening of the nook has vanished. It hasn't been covered over with a thick bush, but it's as if the opening was never there.

It only took a split-second after turning to the sealed nook entrance before turning back to see a pop-eyed woman staring menacingly into their faces. Her dangling tongue drips with saliva all over the front of her shirt as she smiles from ear to ear. The only five teeth in her mouth are rotted to the abscess stage of pus on her brown gums. Her dirty, crumpled skin looks like sagging leather around her face and neck. She slightly resembles Charlena but has less human-like features.

The boys flinch from the hideous sight and make a run toward the edge of the nook. Small, muddy hands reach out of the short shrubbery that squeezes in between the iroko trees and tries to grab them. The boys are trapped.

They turn around to see the woman crouched further toward the ground like a cat sizing them up. She eases closer and closer, salivating as they scamper along the wall that tries to grab them.

Revolving in a constant circle, tiny moans and groans can be heard coming from the bushes, sounding like children in a painful desperation to either feed or break free.

The woman draws within inches when the boys react in desperation and bolt for the shortest area of bushes. Desperate hands reach out from the shrubbery, but the gruesome sight of the woman keeps them charging forward for possible freedom.

Lukozi takes one big leap, and his shirt is snagged by a hand. Without even thinking about the hand that's holding on to Lukozi, Umar leaps into him and breaks the hold while getting grabbed himself.

Lukozi cocks back with the stick that he still wields and starts to take a big swat. It's caught by the old veiny hands of the woman. She pulls the stick that he refuses to let go, and he falls back into the bushes. The hands that were holding on to Umar quickly shifted to grabbing Lukozi's fallen body.

Umar rises out of the bushes and tries to grab his friend before more hands shoot out from the bushes. He jumps with tears in his eyes and makes a run for it.

The desperate cries from Lukozi can be heard while Umar scurries away. "Umar!"

Umar looks back and sees nothing but his friend's legs sliding down to the inside of the bushes as he's being pulled back into the nook. The woman is nowhere in sight, but the fear of the entire area pushes Umar forward as his friend gets taken.

As the old memory diminishes and an older Umar's thoughts come back to the present day, he continues to sit in his darkened office, staring at the photo album.

The bright and sunny outside background that once displayed joyful neighbors walking their dogs and children playing now displays nothing but a sixteen-year-old Lukozi standing on the sidewalk across the street, staring directly through the four inches. He is completely frozen in his desolate existence on the sidewalk.

Umar senses that he's being watched, and his eyes slowly start to shift toward the bright four-inch crack, pulling his head along. He notices his old friend standing on the other side of the street, looking at him menacingly. He thinks to himself whether that's actually his friend and whispers, "Awa ara ko ni pinya."

To Be Continued

www.ingramcontent.com/pod-product-compliance
Lightning Source LLC
Chambersburg PA
CBHW070629310726
48982CB00001B/224